THE
MIST

THE
MIST

STEPHEN KING

Previously published in *Skeleton Crew*

A SIGNET BOOK

SIGNET
Published by New American Library, a division of
Penguin Group (USA) Inc., 375 Hudson Street,
New York, New York 10014, USA
Penguin Group (Canada), 90 Eglinton Avenue East, Suite 700, Toronto,
Ontario M4P 2Y3, Canada (a division of Pearson Penguin Canada Inc.)
Penguin Books Ltd., 80 Strand, London WC2R 0RL, England
Penguin Ireland, 25 St. Stephen's Green, Dublin 2,
Ireland (a division of Penguin Books Ltd.)
Penguin Group (Australia), 250 Camberwell Road, Camberwell, Victoria 3124,
Australia (a division of Pearson Australia Group Pty. Ltd.)
Penguin Books India Pvt. Ltd., 11 Community Centre, Panchsheel Park,
New Delhi - 110 017, India
Penguin Group (NZ), 67 Apollo Drive, Rosedale, North Shore 0745,
Auckland, New Zealand (a division of Pearson New Zealand Ltd.)
Penguin Books (South Africa) (Pty.) Ltd., 24 Sturdee Avenue,
Rosebank, Johannesburg 2196, South Africa

Penguin Books Ltd., Registered Offices:
80 Strand, London WC2R 0RL, England

Published by Signet, an imprint of New American Library, a division of
Penguin Group (USA) Inc. "The Mist" first appeared in *Dark Forces*, edited
by Kirby McCauley. "The Mist" also appeared in *Skeleton Crew*.

First Signet Printing (*The Mist* Movie Tie-in), October 2007
10 9 8 7 6 5 4 3 2 1

Copyright © Stephen King, 1980
All rights reserved

 REGISTERED TRADEMARK—MARCA REGISTRADA

Printed in the United States of America

PUBLISHER'S NOTE
This is a work of fiction. Names, characters, places, and incidents either are
the product of the author's imagination or are used fictitiously, and any
resemblance to actual persons, living or dead, business establishments,
events, or locales is entirely coincidental.
   The publisher does not have any control over and does not assume any
responsibility for author or third-party Web sites or their content.

I

The Coming of the Storm.

This is what happened. On the night that the worst heat wave in northern New England history finally broke—the night of July 19—the entire western Maine region was lashed with the most vicious thunderstorms I have ever seen.

We lived on Long Lake, and we saw the first of the storms beating its way across the water toward us just before dark. For an hour before, the air had been utterly still. The American flag that my father put up on our boathouse in 1936 lay limp against its pole. Not even its hem fluttered. The heat was like a solid thing, and it seemed as deep as sullen quarry-water. That afternoon the three of us had gone swimming, but the water was no relief unless you went out deep. Neither Steffy nor I wanted to go deep because Billy couldn't. Billy is five.

We ate a cold supper at five-thirty, picking listlessly at ham sandwiches and potato salad out on the deck that faces the lake. Nobody seemed to want anything but Pepsi, which was in a steel bucket of ice cubes.

After supper Billy went out back to play on his monkey bars for a while. Steff and I sat without talking much, smoking and looking across the sullen flat mirror of the lake to Harrison on the far side. A few powerboats droned back and forth. The evergreens over there looked dusty and beaten. In the west, great purple thunderheads were slowly building up, massing like an army. Lightning flashed inside them. Next door, Brent Norton's radio, tuned to that classical-music station that broadcasts from the top of Mount Washington, sent out a loud bray of static each time the lightning flashed. Norton was a lawyer from New Jersey and his place on Long Lake was only a summer cottage with no furnace or insulation. Two years before, we had a boundary dispute that finally wound up in county court. I won. Norton claimed I won because he was an out-of-towner. There was no love lost between us.

Steff sighed and fanned the top of her breasts with the edge of her halter. I doubted if it cooled her off much but it improved the view a lot.

"I don't want to scare you," I said, "but there's a bad storm on the way, I think."

She looked at me doubtfully. "There were thunderheads last night and the night before, David. They just broke up."

"They won't do that tonight."

"No?"

"If it gets bad enough, we're going to go downstairs."

"How bad do you think it can get?"

My dad was the first to build a year-round home on this side of the lake. When he was hardly more than a kid, he and his brothers put up a summer place where the house now stood, and in 1938 a summer storm knocked it flat, stone walls and all. Only the boathouse escaped. A year later he started the big house. It's the trees that do the damage in a bad blow. They get old, and the wind knocks them over. It's mother nature's way of cleaning house periodically.

"I don't really know," I said, truthfully enough. I had only heard stories about the great storm of thirty-eight. "But the wind can come off the lake like an express train."

Billy came back a while later, complaining that the monkey bars were no fun because he was "all sweated up." I ruffled his hair and gave him another Pepsi. More work for the dentist.

The thunderheads were getting closer, pushing away the blue. There was no doubt now that a storm was coming. Norton had turned off his radio. Billy sat between his mother and me, watching the sky, fascinated. Thunder boomed, rolling slowly across the lake and then echoing back again. The clouds twisted and rolled, now black, now purple, now veined, now black again. They gradually overspread the lake, and I could see a delicate caul of rain extending down from them. It was still a distance away. As we watched, it was probably raining on Bolster's Mills, or maybe even Norway.

The air began to move, jerkily at first, lifting the flag and then dropping it again. It began to freshen and grew steady, first cooling the perspiration on our bodies and then seeming to freeze it.

That was when I saw the silver veil rolling across the lake. It blotted out Harrison in seconds and then came straight at us. The powerboats had vacated the scene.

Billy stood up from his chair, which was a miniature replica of our director's chairs, complete with his name printed on the back. "Daddy! Look!"

"Let's go in," I said. I stood up and put my arm around his shoulders.

"But do you see it? Dad, what is it?"

"A water-cyclone. Let's go in."

Steff threw a quick, startled glance at my face and then said, "Come on, Billy. Do what your father says."

We went in through the sliding glass doors that give on the living room. I slid the door shut on its track and paused for another look out. The silver veil was three-quarters of the way across the lake. It had resolved itself into a crazily spinning teacup between the lowering black sky and the surface of the water, which had gone the color of lead streaked with white chrome. The lake had begun to look eerily like the ocean, with high waves rolling in and sending spume up from the docks and breakwaters. Out in the middle, big whitecaps were tossing their heads back and forth.

Watching the water-cyclone was hypnotic. It was nearly on top of us when lightning flashed so brightly that it printed everything on my eyes in negative for thirty seconds afterward. The telephone gave out a startled *ting!* and I turned to see my wife and son standing directly in front of the big picture window that gives us a panoramic view of the lake to the northwest.

One of those terrible visions came to me—I think they are reserved exclusively for husbands and fathers—of the picture window blowing in with a low, hard coughing sound and sending jagged arrows of glass into my wife's bare stomach, into my boy's face and neck. The horrors of the Inquisition are nothing compared to the fates your mind can imagine for your loved ones.

I grabbed them both hard and jerked them away. "What the hell are you doing? Get away from there!"

Steff gave me a startled glance. Billy only looked at me as if he had been partially awakened from a deep dream. I led them into the kitchen and hit the light switch. The phone ting-a-linged again.

Then the wind came. It was as if the house had taken off like a 747. It was a high, breathless whistling, sometimes deepening to a bass roar before glissading up to a whooping scream.

"Go downstairs," I told Steff, and now I had to shout to make myself heard. Directly over the house thunder whacked mammoth planks together and Billy shrank against my leg.

"You come too!" Steff yelled back.

I nodded and made shooing gestures. I had to pry Billy off my leg. "Go with your mother. I want to get some candles in case the lights go off."

He went with her, and I started opening cabinets. Candles are funny things, you know. You lay them by every spring, knowing that a summer storm may knock out the power. And when the time comes, they hide.

I was pawing through the fourth cabinet, past the half-ounce of grass that Steff and I bought four years ago and had still not smoked much of, past Billy's wind-up set of chattering teeth from the Auburn Novelty Shop, past the drifts of photos Steffy kept forgetting to glue in our album. I looked under a Sears catalogue and behind a Kewpie doll from Taiwan that I had won at the Fryeburg Fair knocking over wooden milk bottles with tennis balls.

I found the candles behind the Kewpie doll with its glazed dead man's eyes. They were still wrapped in their cellophane. As my hand closed around them the lights went out and the only electricity was the stuff in the sky. The dining room was lit in a series of shutterflashes that were white and purple. Downstairs I heard Billy start to cry and the low murmur of Steff soothing him.

I had to have one more look at the storm.

The water-cyclone had either passed us or broken up when it reached the shoreline, but I still couldn't see twenty yards out onto the lake. The water was in complete turmoil. I saw someone's dock—the Jassers', maybe—hurry by with its main supports alternately turned up to the sky and buried in the churning water.

I went downstairs. Billy ran to me and clung to my legs. I lifted him up and gave him a hug. Then I lit the candles. We sat in the guest room down the hall from my little studio and looked at each other's faces in the flickering yellow glow and listened to the storm roar and bash at our house. About twenty minutes later we heard a ripping, rending crash as one of the big pines went down nearby. Then there was a lull.

"Is it over?" Steff asked.

"Maybe," I said. "Maybe only for a while."

We went upstairs, each of us carrying a candle, like monks going to vespers. Billy carried his proudly and carefully. Carrying a candle, carrying the *fire*, was a very big deal for him. It helped him forget about being afraid.

It was too dark to see what damage had been done around the house. It was past Billy's bedtime, but neither of us suggested putting him in. We sat in the living room, listened to the wind, and looked at the lightning.

About an hour later it began to crank up again. For three weeks the temperature had been over ninety, and on six of those twenty-one days the National Weather Service station at the Portland Jetport had reported temperatures of over one hundred degrees. Queer weather. Coupled with the grueling winter we had come through and the late spring, some people had dragged out that old chestnut about the long-range results of the fifties A-bomb tests again. That, and of course, the end of the world. The oldest chestnut of them all.

The second squall wasn't so hard, but we heard the crash of several trees weakened by the first onslaught. As the wind began to die down again, one thudded heavily on the roof, like a fist dropped on a coffin lid. Billy jumped and looked apprehensively upward.

"It'll hold, champ," I said.

Billy smiled nervously.

Around ten o'clock the last squall came. It was bad. The wind howled almost as loudly as it had the first time, and lightning seemed to be flashing all around us. More trees fell, and there was a splintering crash down by the water that made Steff utter a low cry. Billy had gone to sleep on her lap.

"David, what was that?"

"I think it was the boathouse."

"Oh. Oh, Jesus."

"Steffy, I want us to go downstairs again." I took Billy in my arms and stood up with him. Steff's eyes were big and frightened.

"David, are we going to be all right?"

"Yes."

"Really?"

"Yes."

We went downstairs. Ten minutes later, as the final

squall peaked, there was a splintering crash from upstairs—the picture window. So maybe my vision earlier hadn't been so crazy after all. Steff, who had been dozing, woke up with a little shriek, and Billy stirred uneasily in the guest bed.

"The rain will come in," she said. "It'll ruin the furniture."

"If it does, it does. It's insured."

"That doesn't make it any better," she said in an upset, scolding voice. "Your mother's dresser . . . our new sofa . . . the color TV . . ."

"Shhh," I said. "Go to sleep."

"I can't," she said, and five minutes later she had.

I stayed awake for another half hour with one lit candle for company, listening to the thunder walk and talk outside. I had a feeling that there were going to be a lot of people from the lakefront communities calling their insurance agents in the morning, a lot of chainsaws burring as cottage owners cut up the trees that had fallen on their roofs and battered through their windows, and a lot of orange CMP trucks on the road.

The storm was fading now, with no sign of a new squall coming in. I went back upstairs, leaving Steff and Billy on the bed, and looked into the living room. The sliding glass door had held. But where the picture window had been there was now a jagged hole stuffed with birch leaves. It was the top of the old tree that had stood by our outside basement access for as long as I could remember. Looking at its top, now visiting in our living room, I could understand what Steff had meant by saying insurance didn't make it any better. I had loved that tree. It had been a hard campaigner of many winters, the one tree on the lakeside of the house that was exempt from my own chainsaw. Big chunks of glass on the rug reflected my candle-flame over and over. I reminded myself to warn Steff and Billy. They would want to wear their slippers in here. Both of them liked to slop around barefoot in the morning.

I went downstairs again. All three of us slept together in the guest bed, Billy between Steff and me. I had a dream that I saw God walking across Harrison on the far side of the lake, a God so gigantic that above the waist He was lost in a clear blue sky. In the dream I could hear the rending crack and splinter of breaking trees as God stamped the woods into the shape of His footsteps. He was circling the lake, coming toward the Bridgton side, toward us, and all the houses and cottages and summer places were bursting into purple-white flame like lightning, and soon the smoke covered everything. The smoke covered everything like a mist.

II

After the Storm. Norton. A Trip to Town.

"Jeee-pers," Billy said.

He was standing by the fence that separates our property from Norton's and looking down our driveway. The driveway runs a quarter of a mile to a camp road, which, in its turn, runs about three-quarters of a mile to a stretch of two-lane blacktop, called Kansas Road. From Kansas Road you can go anywhere you want, as long as it's Bridgton.

I saw what Billy was looking at and my heart went cold.

"Don't go any closer, champ. Right there is close enough."

Billy didn't argue.

The morning was bright and as clear as a bell. The sky, which had been a mushy, hazy color during the heat wave, had regained a deep, crisp blue that was nearly autumnal. There was a light breeze, making cheerful sun-dapples move back and forth in the driveway. Not far from where Billy was standing there was a steady hissing noise, and in the grass there was what you might at first have taken for a writhing bundle of snakes. The power lines leading to our house had fallen in an untidy tangle about twenty feet away and lay in a burned patch of grass. They were twisting lazily and spitting. If the trees and grass hadn't been so completely damped down by the torrential rains, the house might have gone up. As it was, there was only that black patch where the wires had touched directly.

"Could that lectercute a person, Daddy?"

"Yeah. It could."

"What are we going to do about it?"

"Nothing. Wait for the CMP."

"When will they come?"

"I don't know." Five-year-olds have as many questions as Hallmark has cards. "I imagine they're pretty busy this morning. Want to take a walk up to the end of the driveway with me?"

He started to come and then stopped, eyeing the wires nervously. One of them humped up and turned over lazily, as if beckoning.

"Daddy, can lectricity shoot through the ground?"

A fair question. "Yes, but don't worry. Electricity wants the ground, not you, Billy. You'll be all right if you stay away from the wires."

"Wants the ground," he muttered, and then came to me. We walked up the driveway holding hands.

It was worse than I had imagined. Trees had fallen across the drive in four different places, one of them small, two of them middling, and one old baby that must have been five feet through the middle. Moss was crusted onto it like a moldy corset.

Branches, some half-stripped of their leaves, lay everywhere in jackstraw profusion. Billy and I walked up to the camp road, tossing the smaller branches off into the woods on either side. It reminded me of a summer's day that had been maybe twenty-five years before; I couldn't have been much older than Billy was now. All my uncles had been here, and they had spent the day in the woods with axes and hatchets and Darcy poles, cutting brush. Later that afternoon they had all sat down to the trestle picnic table my dad and mom used to have and there had been a monster meal of hot dogs and hamburgers and potato salad. The 'Gansett beer had flowed like water and my uncle Reuben took a dive into the lake with all his clothes on, even his deckshoes. In those days there were still deer in these woods.

"Daddy, can I go down to the lake?"

He was tired of throwing branches, and the thing to do with a little boy when he's tired is to let him go do something else. "Sure."

We walked back to the house together and then Billy cut right, going around the house and giving the downed wires a large berth. I went left, into the garage, to get my McCullough. As I had suspected, I could already hear the unpleasant song of the chainsaw up and down the lake.

I topped up the tank, took off my shirt, and was starting back up the driveway when Steff came out.

She eyed the downed trees lying across the driveway nervously.

"How bad is it?"

"I can cut it up. How bad is it in there?"

"Well, I got the glass cleaned up, but you're going to have to do something about that tree, David. We can't have a tree in the living room."

"No," I said. "I guess we can't."

We looked at each other in the morning sunlight and got to giggling. I set the McCullough down on the cement areaway, and kissed her, holding her buttocks firmly.

"Don't," she murmured. "Billy's—"

He came tearing around the corner of the house just then. "Dad! Daddy! Y'oughta see the—"

Steffy saw the live wires and screamed for him to watch out. Billy, who was a good distance away from them, pulled up short and stared at his mother as if she had gone mad.

"I'm okay, Mom," he said in the careful tone of voice you use to placate the very old and senile. He walked toward us, showing us how all right he was, and Steff began to tremble in my arms.

"It's all right," I said in her ear. "He knows about them."

"Yes, but people get killed," she said. "They have ads all the time on television about live wires, people get—Billy, I want you to come in the house right now!"

"Aw, come on, Mom! I wanna show Dad the boathouse!" He was almost bug-eyed with excitement and disappointment. He had gotten a taste of poststorm apocalypse and wanted to share it.

"You go in right now! Those wires are dangerous and—"

"Dad said they want the ground, not me—"

"Billy, don't you argue with me!"

"I'll come down and look, champ. Go on down yourself." I could feel Steff tensing against me. "Go around the other side, kiddo."

"Yeah! Okay!"

He tore past us, taking the stone steps that led around the west end of the house two by two. He disappeared with his shirttail flying, trailing back one word—"Wow!"—as he spotted some other piece of destruction.

"He knows about the wires, Steffy." I took her gently by the shoulders. "He's scared of them. That's good. It makes him safe."

One tear tracked down her cheek. "David, I'm scared."

"Come on! It's over."

"Is it? Last winter . . . and the late spring . . . they called it a black spring in town . . . they said there hadn't been one in these parts since 1888—"

"They" undoubtedly meant Mrs. Carmody, who kept the Bridgton Antiquary, a junk shop that Steff liked to rummage around in sometimes. Billy loved to go with her. In one of the shadowy, dusty back rooms, stuffed owls with gold-ringed eyes spread their wings forever as their feet endlessly grasped varnished logs; stuffed raccoons stood in a trio around a "stream" that was a long fragment of dusty mirror; and one moth-eaten wolf, which was foaming sawdust instead of saliva around his muzzle, snarled a creepy eternal snarl. Mrs. Carmody claimed the wolf was shot by her father as it came to drink from Stevens Brook one September afternoon in 1901.

The expeditions to Mrs. Carmody's Antiquary shop worked well for my wife and son. She was into carnival glass and he was into death in the name of taxidermy. But I thought that the old woman exercised a rather unpleasant hold over Steff's mind, which was in all other ways practical and hardheaded. She had found Steff's vulnerable spot, a mental Achilles' heel. Nor was Steff the only one in town who was fascinated by Mrs. Carmody's gothic pronouncements and folk remedies (which were always prescribed in God's name).

Stump-water would take off bruises if your husband was the sort who got a bit too free with his fists after three drinks. You could tell what kind of a winter was coming by counting the rings on the caterpillars in June or by measuring the thickness of August honeycomb. And now, good God protect and preserve us, THE BLACK SPRING OF 1888 (add your own exclamation points, as many as you think it deserves). I had also heard the story. It's one they like to pass around up here—if the spring is cold enough, the ice on the lakes will eventually turn as black as a rotted tooth. It's rare, but hardly a once-in-a-century occurrence. They like to pass it around, but I doubt that many could pass it around with as much conviction as Mrs. Carmody.

"We had a hard winter and a late spring," I said. "Now we're having a hot summer. And we had a storm but it's over. You're not acting like yourself, Stephanie."

"That wasn't an ordinary storm," she said in that same husky voice.

"No," I said. "I'll go along with you there."

I had heard the Black Spring story from Bill Giosti, who owned and operated—after a fashion—Giosti's Mobil in Casco Village. Bill ran the place with his three tosspot sons (with occasional help from his four tosspot grandsons . . . when they could take time off from tinkering with their snowmobiles and dirtbikes). Bill was seventy, looked eighty, and could still drink like twenty-three when the mood was on him. Billy and I had taken the Scout in for a fill-up the day after a surprise mid-May storm dropped nearly a foot of wet, heavy snow on the region, covering the new grass and flowers. Giosti had been in his cups for fair, and happy to pass along the Black Spring story, along with his own original twist. But we get snow in May sometimes; it comes and it's gone two days later. It's no big deal.

Steff was glancing doubtfully at the downed wires again. "When will the power company come?"

"Just as soon as they can. It won't be long. I just don't want you to worry about Billy. His head's on pretty straight. He forgets to pick up his clothes, but he isn't going to go and step on a bunch of live lines. He's got a good, healthy dose of self-interest." I touched a corner of her mouth and it obliged by turning up in the beginning of a smile. "Better?"

"You always make it seem better," she said, and that made me feel good.

From the lakeside of the house Billy was yelling for us to come and see.

"Come on," I said. "Let's go look at the damage."

She snorted ruefully. "If I want to look at damage, I can go sit in my living room."

"Make a little kid happy, then."

We walked down the stone steps, hand in hand. We had just reached the first turn in them when Billy came from the other direction at speed, almost knocking us over.

"Take it easy," Steff said, frowning a little. Maybe, in her mind, she was seeing him skidding into that deadly nest of live wires instead of the two of us.

"You gotta come see!" Billy panted. "The boat-house is all bashed! There's a dock on the rocks . . . and trees in the boat cove . . . Jesus *Christ!*"

"Billy Drayton!" Steff thundered.

"Sorry, Ma—but you gotta—wow!" He was gone again.

"Having spoken, the doomsayer departs," I said, and that made Steff giggle again. "Listen, after I cut up those trees across the driveway, I'll go by the Central Maine Power office on Portland Road. Tell them what we got. Okay?"

"Okay," she said gratefully. "When do you think you can go?"

Except for the big tree—the one with the moldy corset of moss—it would have been an hour's work. With the big one added in, I didn't think the job would be done until eleven or so.

"I'll give you lunch here, then. But you'll have to get some things at the market for me . . . we're almost out of milk and butter. Also . . . well, I'll have to make you a list."

Give a woman a disaster and she turns squirrel. I gave her a hug and nodded. We went on around the house. It didn't take more than a glance to understand why Billy had been a little overwhelmed.

"Lordy," Steff said in a faint voice.

From where we stood we had enough elevation to be able to see almost a quarter of a mile of shoreline—the Bibber property to our left, our own, and Brent Norton's to our right.

The huge old pine that had guarded our boat cove had been sheared off halfway up. What was left looked like a brutally sharpened pencil, and the inside of the tree seemed a glistening and defenseless white against the age-and-weather-darkened outer bark. A hundred feet of tree, the old pine's top half, lay partly submerged in our shallow cove. It occurred to me that we were very lucky our little Star-Cruiser wasn't sunk underneath it. The week before, it had developed engine trouble and it was still at the Naples marina, patiently waiting its turn.

On the other side of our little piece of shorefront, the boathouse my father had built—the boathouse that had once housed a sixty-foot Chris-Craft when the Drayton family fortunes had been at a higher mark than they were today—lay under another big tree. It was the one that had stood on Norton's side of the property line, I saw. That raised the first flush of anger. The tree had been dead for five years and he should have long since had it taken down. Now it was three-quarters of the way down; our boathouse was propping it up. The roof had taken on a drunken, swaybacked look. The wind had swirled shingles from the hole the tree had made all over the point of land the boathouse stood on. Billy's description, "bashed," was as good as any.

"That's Norton's tree!" Steff said. And she said it with such hurt indignation that I had to smile in spite of the pain I felt. The flagpole was lying in the water and Old Glory floated soggily beside it in a tangle of lanyard. And I could imagine Norton's response: Sue me.

Billy was on the rock breakwater, examining the dock that had washed up on the stones. It was painted in jaunty blue and yellow stripes. He looked back over his shoulder at us and yelled gleefully, "It's the Marlinses', isn't it?"

"Yeah, it is," I said. "Wade in and fish the flag out, would you, Big Bill?"

"Sure!"

To the right of the breakwater was a small sandy beach. In 1941, before Pearl Harbor paid off the Great

Depression in blood, my dad hired a man to truck in that fine beach sand—six dumptrucks full—and to spread it out to a depth that is about nipple-high on me, say five feet. The workman charged eighty bucks for the job, and the sand has never moved. Just as well, you know, you can't put a sandy beach in on your land now. Now that the sewerage runoff from the booming cottage-building industry has killed most of the fish and made the rest of them unsafe to eat, the EPA has forbidden installing sand beaches. They might upset the ecology of the lake, you see, and it is presently against the law for anyone except land developers to do that.

Billy went for the flag—then stopped. At the same moment I felt Steff go rigid against me, and I saw it myself. The Harrison side of the lake was gone. It had been buried under a line of bright white mist, like a fair-weather cloud fallen to earth.

My dream of the night before recurred, and when Steff asked me what it was, the word that nearly jumped first from my mouth was *God*.

"David?"

You couldn't see even a hint of the shoreline over there, but years of looking at Long Lake made me believe that the shoreline wasn't hidden by much; only yards, maybe. The edge of the mist was nearly ruler-straight.

"What is it, Dad?" Billy yelled. He was in the water up to his knees, groping for the soggy flag.

"Fogbank," I said.

"On the *lake?*" Steff asked doubtfully, and I could

see Mrs. Carmody's influence in her eyes. Damn the woman. My own moment of unease was passing. Dreams, after all, are insubstantial things, like mist itself.

"Sure. You've seen fog on the lake before."

"Never like that. That looks more like a cloud."

"It's the brightness of the sun," I said. "It's the same way clouds look from an airplane when you fly over them."

"What would do it? We only get fog in damp weather."

"No, we've got it right now," I said. "Harrison does, anyway. It's a little leftover from the storm, that's all. Two fronts meeting. Something along that line."

"David, are you sure?"

I laughed and hauled my arm around her neck. "No, actually, I'm bullshitting like crazy. If I was sure, I'd be doing the weather on the six-o'clock news. Go on and make your shopping list."

She gave me one more doubtful glance, looked at the fogbank for a moment or two with the flat of her hand held up to shade her eyes, and then shook her head. "Weird," she said, and walked away.

For Billy, the mist had lost its novelty. He had fished the flag and a tangle of lanyard out of the water. We spread it on the lawn to dry.

"I heard it was wrong to ever let the flag touch the ground, Daddy," he said in a businesslike, let's-get-this-out-of-the-way tone.

"Yeah?"

"Yeah. Victor McAllister says they lectercute people for it."

"Well, you tell Vic he's full of what makes the grass grow green."

"Horseshit, right?" Billy is a bright boy, but oddly humorless. To the champ, everything is serious business. I'm hoping that he'll live long enough to learn that in this world that is a very dangerous attitude.

"Yeah, right, but don't tell your mother I said so. When the flag's dry, we'll put it away. We'll even fold it into a cocked hat, so we'll be on safe ground there."

"Daddy, will we fix the boathouse roof and get a new flagpole?" For the first time he looked anxious. He'd maybe had enough destruction for a while.

I clapped him on the shoulder. "You're damn tooting."

"Can I go over to the Bibbers' and see what happened there?"

"Just for a couple of minutes. They'll be cleaning up, too, and sometimes that makes people feel a little ugly." The way I presently felt about Norton.

"Okay. Bye!" He was off.

"Stay out of their way, champ. And, Billy?"

He glanced back.

"Remember about the live wires. If you see more, steer clear of them."

"Sure, Dad."

I stood there for a moment, first surveying the damage, then glancing out at the mist again. It seemed closer, but it was very hard to tell for sure.

If it was closer, it was defying all the laws of nature, because the wind—a very gentle breeze—was against it. That, of course, was patently impossible. It was very, very white. The only thing I can compare it to would be fresh-fallen snow lying in dazzling contrast to the deep blue brilliance of the winter sky. But snow reflects hundreds and hundreds of diamond points in the sun, and this peculiar fogbank, although bright and clean-looking, did not sparkle. In spite of what Steff had said, mist isn't uncommon on clear days, but when there's a lot of it, the suspended moisture almost always causes a rainbow. But there was no rainbow here.

The unease was back, tugging at me, but before it could deepen, I heard a low mechanical sound—*whut-whut-whut!*—followed by a barely audible "Shit!" The mechanical sound was repeated, but this time there was no oath. The third time the chuffing sound was followed by "Mother-fuck!" in that same low I'm-all-by-myself-but-boy-am-I-pissed tone.

Whut-whut-whut-whut—

—Silence—

—then: "You cunt."

I began to grin. Sound carries well out here, and all the buzzing chainsaws were fairly distant. Distant enough for me to recognize the not-so-dulcet tones of my next-door neighbor, the renowned lawyer and lakefront-property-owner, Brenton Norton.

I moved down a little closer to the water, pretending to stroll toward the dock beached on our breakwater. Now I could see Norton. He was in the clearing beside his screened-in porch, standing on a carpet of old pine needles and dressed in paint-spotted jeans and a white strappy T-shirt. His forty-dollar haircut was in disarray and sweat poured down his face. He was down on one knee, laboring over his own chainsaw. It was much bigger and fancier than my little $79.95 Value House job. It seemed to have everything, in fact, but a starter button. He was yanking a cord, producing the listless *whut-whut-whut* sounds and nothing more. I was gladdened in my heart to see that a yellow birch had fallen across his picnic table and smashed it in two.

Norton gave a tremendous yank on the starter cord.

Whut-whut-whutwhutwhut-WHAT! WHAT! WHAT!...
WHAT! . . . Whut.

Almost had it there for a minute, fella.

Another Herculean tug.

Whut-whut-whut.

"Cocksucker," Norton whispered fiercely, and bared his teeth at his fancy chainsaw.

I went back around the house, feeling really good for the first time since I got up. My own saw started on the first tug, and I went to work.

Around ten o'clock there was a tap on my shoulder. It was Billy with a can of beer in one hand and Steff's list in the other. I stuffed the list in the back pocket of my jeans and took the beer, which was not exactly frosty-cold but at least cool. I chugged almost half of it at once—rarely does a beer taste that good—

and tipped the can in salute at Billy. "Thanks, champ."

"Can I have some?"

I let him have a swallow. He grimaced and handed the can back. I offed the rest and just caught myself as I started to crunch it up in the middle. The deposit law on bottles and cans has been in effect for over three years, but old ways die hard.

"She wrote something across the bottom of the list, but I can't read her writing," Billy said.

I took out the list again. "I can't get WOXO on the radio," Steff's note read. "Do you think the storm knocked them off the air?"

WOXO is the local automated FM rock outlet. It broadcast from Norway, about twenty miles north, and was all that our old and feeble FM receiver would haul in.

"Tell her probably," I said, after reading the question over to him. "Ask her if she can get Portland on the AM band."

"Okay, Daddy, can I come when you go to town?"

"Sure. You and Mommy both, if you want."

"Okay." He ran back to the house with the empty can.

I had worked my way up to the big tree. I made my first cut, sawed through, then turned the saw off for a few moments to let it cool down—the tree was really too big for it, but I thought it would be all right if I didn't rush it. I wondered if the dirt road leading up to Kansas Road was clear of falls, and just as I was wondering, an orange CMP truck lumbered past, probably on its way to the far end of our little road. So that was all right. The road was clear and the power guys would be here by noon to take care of the live lines.

I cut a big chunk off the tree, dragged it to the side of the driveway, and tumbled it over the edge. It rolled down the slope and into the underbrush that had crept back since the long-ago day when my dad and his brothers—all of them artists; we have always been an artistic family, the Draytons—had cleared it away.

I wiped sweat off my face with my arm and wished for another beer; one really only sets your mouth. I picked up the chainsaw and thought about WOXO being off the air. That was the direction that funny fogbank had come from. And it was the direction Shaymore (pronounced *Shammore* by the locals) lay in. Shaymore was where the Arrowhead Project was.

That was old Bill Giosti's theory about the so-called Black Spring: the Arrowhead Project. In the western part of Shaymore, not far from where the town borders on Stoneham, there was a small government preserve surrounded with wire. There were sentries and closed-circuit television cameras and God knew what else. Or so I had heard; I'd never actually seen it, although the Old Shaymore Road runs along the eastern side of the government land for a mile or so.

No one knew for sure where the name Arrowhead Project came from and no one could tell you for one hundred percent sure that that really was the name of the project—if there was a project. Bill Giosti said there was, but when you asked him how and where he came by his information, he got vague. His niece, he said, worked for the Continental Phone Company, and she had heard things. It got like that.

"Atomic things," Bill said that day, leaning in the Scout's window and blowing a healthy draft of Pabst into my face. "That's what they're fooling around with up there. Shooting atoms into the air and all that."

"Mr. Giosti, the air's full of atoms," Billy had said. "That's what Mrs. Neary says. Mrs. Neary says everything's full of atoms."

Bill Giosti gave my son Bill a long, bloodshot glance that finally deflated him. "These are *different* atoms, son."

"Oh, yeah," Billy muttered, giving in.

Dick Muehler, our insurance agent, said the Arrowhead Project was an agricultural station the government was running, no more or less. "Bigger tomatoes with a longer growing season," Dick said sagely, and then went back to showing me how I could help my family most efficiently by dying young. Janine Lawless, our postlady, said it was a geological survey having something to do with shale oil. She knew for a fact, because her husband's brother worked for a man who had—

Mrs. Carmody, now . . . she probably leaned more to Bill Giosti's view of the matter. Not just atoms, but *different* atoms.

I cut two more chunks off the big tree and dropped

them over the side before Billy came back with a fresh beer in one hand and a note from Steff in the other. If there's anything Big Bill likes to do more than run messages, I don't know what it could be.

"Thanks," I said, taking them both.

"Can I have a swallow?"

"Just one. You took two last time. Can't have you running around drunk at ten in the morning."

"Quarter past," he said, and smiled shyly over the top of the can. I smiled back—not that it was such a great joke, you know, but Billy makes them so rarely—and then read the note.

"Got JBQ on the radio," Steffy had written. "Don't get drunk before you go to town. You can have one more, but that's it before lunch. Do you think you can get up our road okay?"

I handed him the note back and took my beer. "Tell her the road's okay because a power truck just went by. They'll be working their way up here."

"Okay."

"Champ?"

"What, Dad?"

"Tell her everything's okay."

He smiled again, maybe telling himself first. "Okay."

He ran back and I watched him go, legs pumping, soles of his zori showing. I love him. It's his face and sometimes the way his eyes turn up to mine that make me feel as if things are really okay. It's a lie, of course—things are not okay and never have been—but my kid makes me believe the lie.

I drank some beer, set the can down carefully on a rock, and got the chainsaw going again. About twenty minutes later I felt a light tap on my shoulder and turned, expecting to see Billy again. Instead it was Brent Norton. I turned off the chainsaw.

He didn't look the way Norton usually looks. He looked hot and tired and unhappy and a little bewildered.

"Hi, Brent," I said. Our last words had been hard ones, and I was a little unsure how to proceed. I had a funny feeling that he had been standing behind me for the last five minutes or so, clearing his throat decorously under the chainsaw's aggressive roar. I hadn't gotten a really good look at him this summer. He had lost weight, but it didn't look good. It should have, because he had been carrying around an extra twenty pounds, but it didn't. His wife had died the previous November. Cancer. Aggie Bibber told Steffy that. Aggie was our resident necrologist. Every neighborhood has one. From the casual way Norton had of ragging his wife and belittling her (doing it with the contemptuous ease of a veteran matador inserting *banderillas* in an old bull's lumbering body), I would have guessed he'd be glad to have her gone. If asked, I might even have speculated that he'd show up this summer with a girl twenty years younger than he was on his arm and a silly my-cock-has-died-and-gone-to-heaven grin on his face. But instead of the silly grin there was only a new batch of age lines, and the weight had come off in all the wrong places, leaving sags and folds and dewlaps that told their own story. For one passing moment I wanted only to lead Norton to a patch of sun and sit him beside one of the fallen trees with my can of beer in his hand, and do a charcoal sketch of him.

"Hi, Dave," he said, after a long moment of awkward silence—a silence that was made even louder by the absence of the chainsaw's racket and roar. He stopped, then blurted: "That tree. That damn tree. I'm sorry. You were right."

I shrugged.

He said, "Another tree fell on my car."

"I'm sorry to h—" I began, and then a horrid suspicion dawned. "It wasn't the T-Bird, was it?"

"Yeah. It was."

Norton had a 1960 Thunderbird in mint condition, only thirty thousand miles. It was a deep midnight blue inside and out. He drove it only summers, and then only rarely. He loved that Bird the way some men love electric trains or model ships or target-shooting pistols.

"That's a bitch," I said, and meant it.

He shook his head slowly. "I almost didn't bring it up. Almost brought the station wagon, you know. Then I said what the hell. I drove it up and a big old rotten pine fell on it. The roof of it's all bashed in. And I thought I'd cut it up . . . the tree, I mean . . . but I can't get my chainsaw to fire up . . . I paid two hundred dollars for that sucker . . . and . . . and . . ."

His throat began to emit little clicking sounds. His mouth worked as if he were toothless and chewing dates. For one helpless second I thought he was going to just stand there and bawl like a kid on a sandlot. Then he got himself under some halfway kind of control, shrugged, and turned away as if to look at the chunks of wood I had cut up.

"Well, we can look at your saw," I said. "Your T-Bird insured?"

"Yeah," he said, "like your boathouse."

I saw what he meant, and remembered again what Steff had said about insurance.

"Listen, Dave, I wondered if I could borrow your Saab and take a run up to town. I thought I'd get some bread and cold cuts and beer. A lot of beer."

"Billy and I are going up in the Scout," I said. "Come with us if you want. That is, if you'll give me a hand dragging the rest of this tree off to one side."

"Happy to."

He grabbed one end but couldn't quite lift it up. I had to do most of the work. Between the two of us we were able to tumble it into the underbrush. Norton was puffing and panting, his cheeks nearly purple. After all the yanking he had done on that chainsaw starter pull, I was a little worried about his ticker.

"Okay?" I asked, and he nodded, still breathing fast. "Come on back to the house, then. I can fix you up with a beer."

"Thank you," he said. "How is Stephanie?" He was regaining some of the old smooth pomposity that I disliked.

"Very well, thanks."

"And your son?"

"He's fine, too."

"Glad to hear it."

Steff came out, and a moment's surprise passed over her face when she saw who was with me. Norton smiled and his eyes crawled over her tight T-shirt. He hadn't changed that much after all.

"Hello, Brent," she said cautiously. Billy poked his head out from under her arm.

"Hello, Stephanie. Hi, Billy."

"Brent's T-Bird took a pretty good rap in the storm," I told her. "Stove in the roof, he says."

"Oh, no!"

Norton told it again while he drank one of our beers. I was sipping a third, but I had no kind of buzz on; apparently I had sweat the beer out as rapidly as I drank it.

"He's going to come to town with Billy and me."

"Well, I won't expect you for a while. You may have to go to the Shop-and-Save in Norway."

"Oh? Why?"

"Well, if the power's off in Bridgton—"

"Mom says all the cash registers and things run on electricity," Billy supplied.

It was a good point.

"Have you still got the list?"

I patted my hip pocket.

Her eyes shifted to Norton. "I'm very sorry about Carla, Brent. We all were."

"Thank you," he said. "Thank you very much."

There was another moment of awkward silence which Billy broke. "Can we go now, Daddy?" He had changed to jeans and sneakers.

"Yeah, I guess so. You ready, Brent?"

"Give me another beer for the road and I will be."

Steffy's brow creased. She had never approved of the one-for-the-road philosophy, or of men who drive with a can of Bud leaning against their crotches. I gave her a bare nod and she shrugged. I didn't want to reopen things with Norton now. She got him a beer.

"Thanks," he said to Steffy, not really thanking her but only mouthing a word. It was the way you thank a waitress in a restaurant. He turned back to me. "Lead on, Macduff."

"Be right with you," I said, and went into the living room.

Norton followed, and exclaimed over the birch, but I wasn't interested in that or in the cost of replacing the window just then. I was looking at the lake through the sliding glass panel that gave on our deck. The breeze had freshened a little and the day had warmed up five degrees or so while I was cutting wood. I thought the odd mist we'd noticed earlier would surely have broken up, but it hadn't. It was closer, too. Halfway across the lake now.

"I noticed that earlier," Norton said, pontificating. "Some kind of temperature inversion, that's my guess."

I didn't like it. I felt very strongly that I had never seen a mist exactly like this one. Part of it was the unnerving straight edge of its leading front. Nothing in nature is that even; man is the inventor of straight edges. Part of it was that pure, dazzling whiteness, with no variation but also without the sparkle of moisture. It was only half a mile or so off now, and the contrast between it and the blues of the lake and sky was more striking than ever.

"Come on, Dad!" Billy was tugging at my pants.

We all went back to the kitchen. Brent Norton spared one final glance at the tree that had crashed into our living room.

"Too bad it wasn't an apple tree, huh?" Billy remarked brightly. "That's what my mom said. Pretty funny, don't you think?"

"Your mother's a real card, Billy," Norton said. He ruffled Billy's hair in a perfunctory way and his eyes went to the front of Steff's T-shirt again. No, he was not a man I was ever going to be able to really like.

"Listen, why don't you come with us, Steff?" I asked. For no concrete reason I suddenly wanted her to come along.

"No, I think I'll stay here and pull some weeds in the garden," she said. Her eyes shifted toward Norton and then back to me. "This morning it seems like I'm the only thing around here that doesn't run on electricity."

Norton laughed too heartily.

I was getting her message, but tried one more time. "You sure?"

"Sure," she said firmly. "The old bend-and-stretch will do me good."

"Well, don't get too much sun."

"I'll put on my straw hat. We'll have sandwiches when you get back."

"Good."

She turned her face up to be kissed. "Be careful. There might be blowdowns on Kansas Road too, you know."

"I'll be careful."

"You be careful, too," she told Billy, and kissed his cheek.

"Right, Mom." He banged out of the door and the screen cracked shut behind him.

Norton and I walked out after him. "Why don't we go over to your place and cut the tree off your Bird?" I asked him. All of a sudden I could think of lots of reasons to delay leaving for town.

"I don't even want to look at it until after lunch and a few more of these," Norton said, holding up his beer can. "The damage has been done, Dave old buddy."

I didn't like him calling me buddy, either.

We all got into the front seat of the Scout (in the far corner of the garage my scarred Fisher plow blade sat glimmering yellow, like the ghost of Christmas yet-to-come) and I backed out, crunching over a litter of storm-blown twigs. Steff was standing on the cement path which leads to the vegetable patch at the extreme west end of our property. She had a pair of clippers in one gloved hand and the weeding claw in the other. She had put on her old floppy sunhat, and it cast a band of shadow over her face. I tapped

the horn twice, lightly, and she raised the hand holding the clippers in answer. We pulled out. I haven't
seen my wife since then.

We had to stop once on our way up to Kansas
Road. Since the power truck had driven through, a
pretty fair-sized pine had dropped across the road.
Norton and I got out and moved it enough so I could
inch the Scout by, getting our hands all pitchy in the
process. Billy wanted to help but I waved him back.
I was afraid he might get poked in the eye. Old trees
have always reminded me of the Ents in Tolkien's
wonderful Rings saga, only Ents that have gone bad.
Old trees want to hurt you. It doesn't matter if you're
snowshoeing, cross-country skiing, or just taking a
walk in the woods. Old trees want to hurt you, and
I think they'd kill you if they could.

Kansas Road itself was clear, but in several places
we saw more lines down. About a quarter-mile past
the Vicki-Linn Campground there was a power pole
lying full-length in the ditch, heavy wires snarled
around its top like wild hair.

"That was some storm," Norton said in his mel-
lifluous, courtroom-trained voice; but he didn't seem
to be pontificating now, only solemn.

"Yeah, it was."

"Look, Dad!"

He was pointing at the remains of the Ellitches'
barn. For twelve years it had been sagging tiredly in
Tommy Ellitch's back field, up to its hips in sun-
flowers, goldenrod, and Lolly-come-see-me. Every

fall I would think it could not last through another winter. And every spring it would still be there. But it wasn't anymore. All that remained was a splintered wreckage and a roof that had been mostly stripped of shingles. Its number had come up. And for some reason that echoed solemnly, even ominously, inside me. The storm had come and smashed it flat.

Norton drained his beer, crushed the can in one hand, and dropped it indifferently to the floor of the Scout. Billy opened his mouth to say something and then closed it again—good boy. Norton came from New Jersey, where there was no bottle-and-can law; I guess he could be forgiven for squashing my nickel when I could barely remember not to do it myself.

Billy started fooling with the radio, and I asked him to see if WOXO was back on the air. He dialed up to FM 92 and got nothing but a blank hum. He looked at me and shrugged. I thought for a moment. What other stations were on the far side of that peculiar fog front?

"Try WBLM," I said.

He dialed down to the other end, passing WJBQ-FM and WIGY-FM on the way. They were there, doing business as usual . . . but WBLM, Maine's premier progressive-rock station, was off the air.

"Funny," I said.

"What's that?" Norton asked.

"Nothing. Just thinking out loud."

Billy had tuned back to the musical cereal on WJBQ. Pretty soon we got to town.

The Norge Washateria in the shopping center was closed, it being impossible to run a coin-op laundry without electricity, but both the Bridgton Pharmacy and the Federal Foods Supermarket were open. The parking lot was pretty full, and as always in the middle of the summer, a lot of the cars had out-of-state plates. Little knots of people stood here and there in the sun, noodling about the storm, women with women, men with men.

I saw Mrs. Carmody, she of the stuffed animals and the stump-water lore. She sailed into the supermarket decked out in an amazing canary yellow pantsuit. A purse that looked the size of a small Samsonite suitcase was slung over one forearm. Then an idiot on a Yamaha roared past me, missing my front bumper by a few scant inches. He wore a denim jacket, mirror sunglasses, and no helmet.

"Look at that stupid shit," Norton growled.

I circled the parking lot once, looking for a good space. There were none. I was just resigning myself to a long walk from the far end of the lot when I got lucky. A lime green Cadillac the size of a small cabin cruiser was easing out of a slot in the rank closest to the market's doors. The moment it was gone, I slid into the space.

I gave Billy Steff's shopping list. He was five, but he could read printing. "Get a cart and get started. I want to give your mother a jingle. Mr. Norton will help you. And I'll be right along."

We got out and Billy immediately grabbed Mr. Norton's hand. He'd been taught not to cross the parking lot without holding an adult's hand when he was younger and hadn't yet lost the habit. Norton looked surprised for a moment, and then smiled a little. I could almost forgive him for feeling Steff up with his eyes. The two of them went into the market.

I strolled over to the pay phone, which was on the wall between the drugstore and the Norge. A sweltering woman in a purple sunsuit was jogging the cutoff switch up and down. I stood behind her with my hands in my pockets, wondering why I felt so uneasy about Steff, and why the unease should be all wrapped up with that line of white but unsparkling fog, the radio stations that were off the air . . . and the Arrowhead Project.

The woman in the purple sunsuit had a sunburn and freckles on her fat shoulders. She looked like a sweaty orange baby. She slammed the phone back down in its cradle, turned toward the drugstore and saw me there.

"Save your dime," she said. "Just dah-dah-dah." She walked grumpily away.

I almost slapped my forehead. The phone lines were down someplace, of course. Some of them were underground, but nowhere near all of them. I tried the phone anyway. The pay phones in the area are what Steff calls Paranoid Pay Phones. Instead of putting your dime right in, you get a dial tone and make your call. When someone answers, there's an automatic cutoff and you have to shove your dime in before your party hangs up. They're irritating, but that day it did save me my dime. There was no dial tone. As the lady had said, it was just dah-dah-dah.

I hung up and walked slowly toward the market, just in time to see an amusing little incident. An elderly couple walked toward the IN door, chatting together. And still chatting, they walked right into it. They stopped talking in a jangle and the woman squawked her surprise. They stared at each other comically. Then they laughed, and the old guy pushed the door open for his wife with some effort—those electric-eye doors are heavy—and they went in. When the electricity goes off, it catches you in a hundred different ways.

I pushed the door open myself and noticed the lack of air-conditioning first thing. Usually in the summer they have it cranked up high enough to give you frostbite if you stay in the market more than an hour at a stretch.

Like most modern markets, the Federal was constructed like a Skinner box—modern marketing techniques turn all customers into white rats. The stuff you really needed, staples, like bread, milk, meat, beer, and frozen dinners, was all on the far side of the store. To get there you had to walk past all the impulse items known to modern man—everything from Cricket lighters to rubber dog bones.

Beyond the IN door is the fruit-and-vegetable aisle. I looked up it, but there was no sign of Norton or my son. The old lady who had run into the door was examining the grapefruits. Her husband had produced a net sack to store purchases in.

I walked up the aisle and went left. I found them in the third aisle, Billy mulling over the ranks of Jello-O packages and instant puddings. Norton was standing directly behind him, peering at Steff's list. I had to grin a little at his nonplussed expression.

I threaded my way down to them, past half-loaded carriages (Steff hadn't been the only one struck by the squirreling impulse, apparently) and browsing shoppers. Norton took two cans of pie filling down from the top shelf and put them in the cart.

"How are you doing?" I asked, and Norton looked around with unmistakable relief.

"All right, aren't we, Billy?"

"Sure," Billy said, and couldn't resist adding in a rather smug tone: "But there's lots of stuff Mr. Norton can't read either, Dad."

"Let me see." I took the list.

Norton had made a neat, lawyerly check beside each of the items he and Billy had picked up—half a dozen or so, including the milk and a six-pack of Coke. There were maybe ten other things that she wanted.

"We ought to go back to the fruits and vegetables," I said. "She wants some tomatoes and cucumbers."

Billy started to turn the cart around and Norton said, "You ought to go have a look at the checkout, Dave."

I went and had a look. It was the sort of thing you sometimes see photos of in the paper on a slow newsday, with a humorous caption beneath. Only two lanes were open, and the double line of people waiting to check their purchases out stretched past the mostly denuded bread racks, then made a jig to the right and went out of sight along the frozen-food coolers. All of the new computerized NCRs were hooded. At each of the two open positions, a harried-looking girl was totting up purchases on a battery-powered pocket calculator. Standing with each girl was one of the Federal's two managers, Bud Brown and Ollie Weeks. I liked Ollie but didn't care much for Bud Brown, who seemed to fancy himself the Charles de Gaulle of the supermarket world.

As each girl finished checking her order, Bud or Ollie would paperclip a chit to the customer's cash or check and toss it into the box he was using as a cash repository. They all looked hot and tired.

"Hope you brought a good book," Norton said, joining me. "We're going to be in line for a while."

I thought of Steff again, at home alone, and had another flash of unease. "You go on and get your stuff," I said. "Billy and I can handle the rest of this."

"Want me to grab a few more beers for you too?"

I thought about it, but in spite of the rapprochement, I didn't want to spend the afternoon with Brent Norton getting drunk. Not with the mess things were in around the house.

"Sorry," I said. "I've got to take a raincheck, Brent."

I thought his face stiffened a little. "Okay," he said shortly, and walked off. I watched him go, and then Billy was tugging at my shirt.

"Did you talk to Mommy?"

"Nope. The phone wasn't working. Those lines are down too, I guess."

"Are you worried about her?"

"No," I said, lying. I was worried, all right, but had no idea why I should be. "No, of course I'm not. Are you?"

"No-ooo . . ." But he was. His face had a pinched look. We should have gone back then. But even then it might have been too late.

III

The Coming of the Mist.

We worked our way back to the fruits and vegetables like salmon fighting their way upstream. I saw some familiar faces—Mike Hatlen, one of our selectmen, Mrs. Reppler from the grammar school (she who had terrified generations of third-graders was currently sneering at the cantaloupes), Mrs. Turman, who sometimes sat Billy when Steff and I went out—but mostly they were summer people stocking up on no-cook items and joshing each other about "roughing it." The cold cuts had been picked over as thoroughly as the dimebook tray at a rummage sale; there was nothing left but a few packages of bologna, some macaroni loaf, and one lonely, phallic kielbasa sausage.

I got tomatoes, cukes, and a jar of mayonnaise. She wanted bacon, but all the bacon was gone. I picked up some of the bologna as a substitute, although I've never been able to eat the stuff with any real enthusiasm since the FDA reported that each package contained a small amount of insect filth—a little something extra for your money.

"Look," Billy said as we rounded the corner into the fourth aisle. "There's some army guys."

There were two of them, their dun uniforms standing out against the much brighter background of summer clothes and sportswear. We had gotten used to seeing a scattering of army personnel with the Arrowhead Project only thirty miles or so away. These two looked hardly old enough to shave yet.

I glanced back down at Steff's list and saw that we had everything . . . no, almost but not quite. At the bottom, as an afterthought, she had scribbled: *Bottle of Lancers?* That sounded good to me. A couple of glasses of wine tonight after Billy had sacked out, then maybe a long slow bout of lovemaking before sleep.

I left the cart and worked my way down to the wine and got a bottle. As I walked back I passed the big double doors leading to the storage area and heard the steady roar of a good-sized generator.

I decided it was probably just big enough to keep the cold cases cold, but not large enough to power the doors and cash registers and all the other electrical equipment. It sounded like a motorcycle back there.

Norton appeared just as we got into line, balancing two six-packs of Schlitz Light, a loaf of bread, and the kielbasa I had spotted a few minutes earlier. He got in line with Billy and me. It seemed very warm in the market with the air-conditioning off, and I wondered why none of the stockboys had at least chocked the doors open. I had seen Buddy Eagleton in his red apron two aisles back, doing nothing and piling it up. The generator roared monotonously. I had the beginnings of a headache.

"Put your stuff in here before you drop something," I said.

"Thanks."

The lines were up past the frozen food now; people had to cut through to get what they wanted and there was much excuse-me-ing and pardon-me-ing. "This is going to be a cunt," Norton said morosely, and I frowned a little. That sort of language is rougher than I'd like Billy to hear.

The generator's roar muted a little as the line shuffled forward. Norton and I made desultory conversation, skirting around the ugly property dispute that had landed us in district court and sticking with things like the Red Sox chances and the weather. At last we exhausted our little store of small talk and fell silent. Billy fidgeted beside me. The line crawled along. Now we had frozen dinners on our right and the more expensive wines and champagnes on our left. As the line progressed down to the cheaper wines, I toyed briefly with the idea of picking up a bottle of Ripple, the wine of my flaming youth. I didn't do it. My youth never flamed that much anyway.

"Jeez, why can't they hurry up, Dad?" Billy asked. That pinched look was still on his face, and suddenly, briefly, the mist of disquiet that had settled over me rifted, and something terrible peered through from the other side—the bright and metallic face of terror. Then it passed.

"Keep cool, champ," I said.

We had made it up to the bread racks—to the point where the double line bent to the left. We could see the checkout lanes now, the two that were open and the other four, deserted, each with a little sign on the stationary conveyor belt, signs that read PLEASE CHOOSE ANOTHER LANE and WINSTON. Beyond the lanes was the big sectioned plate-glass window which gave a view of the parking lot and the intersection of Routes 117 and 302 beyond. The view was partially obscured by the white-paper backs of signs advertising current specials and the latest giveaway, which happened to be a set of books called *The Mother Nature Encyclopedia*. We were in the line that would eventually lead us to the checkout where Bud Brown was standing. There were still maybe thirty people in front of us. The easiest one to pick out was Mrs. Carmody in her blazing yellow pantsuit. She looked like an advertisement for yellow fever.

Suddenly a shrieking noise began in the distance. It quickly built up in volume and resolved itself into the crazy warble of a police siren. A horn blared at the intersection and there was a shriek of brakes and burning rubber. I couldn't see—the angle was all wrong—but the siren reached its loudest as it approached the market and then began to fade as the police car went past. A few people broke out of line to look, but not many. They had waited too long to chance losing their places.

Norton went; his stuff was tucked into my cart. After a few moments he came back and got into line again. "Local fuzz," he said.

Then the town fire whistle began to wail, slowly cranking up to a shriek of its own, falling off, then rising again. Billy grabbed my hand—clutched it. "What is it, Daddy?" he asked, and then, immediately: "Is Mommy all right?"

"Must be a fire on the Kansas Road," Norton said. "Those damned live lines from the storm. The fire trucks will go through in a minute."

That gave my disquiet something to crystallize on. There were live lines down in *our* yard.

Bud Brown said something to the checker he was supervising; she had been craning around to see what was happening. She flushed and began to run her calculator again.

I didn't want to be in this line. All of a sudden I very badly didn't want to be in it. But it was moving again, and it seemed foolish to leave now. We had gotten down by the cartons of cigarettes.

Someone pushed through the IN door, some teenager. I think it was the kid we almost hit coming in, the one on the Yamaha with no helmet. "The fog!" he yelled. "Y'oughta see the fog! It's rolling right up Kansas Road!" People looked around at him. He was panting, as if he had run a long distance. Nobody said anything. "Well, y'oughta see it," he repeated, sounding defensive this time. People eyed him and some of them shuffled, but no one wanted to lose his or her place in line. A few people who hadn't reached the lines yet left their carts and strolled through the empty checkout lanes to see if they could see what he was talking about. A big guy in a summer hat with a paisley band (the kind of hat you almost never see except in beer commercials with backyard barbecues as their settings) yanked open the OUT door and several people—ten, maybe a dozen—went out with him. The kid went along.

"Don't let out all the air-conditioning," one of the army kids cracked, and there were a few chuckles. I wasn't chuckling. I had seen the mist coming across the lake.

"Billy, why don't you go have a look?" Norton said.

"No," I said at once, for no concrete reason.

The line moved forward again. People craned their necks, looking for the fog the kid had mentioned, but there was nothing on view except bright blue sky. I heard someone say that the kid must have been joking. Someone else responded that he had seen a funny line of mist on Long Lake not an hour ago. The first whistle whooped and screamed. I didn't like it. It sounded like big-league doom blowing that way.

More people went out. A few even left their places in line, which speeded up the proceedings a bit. Then grizzled old John Lee Frovin, who works as a mechanic at the Texaco station, came ducking in and yelled: "Hey! Anybody got a camera?" He looked around, then ducked back out again.

That caused something of a rush. If it was worth taking a picture of, it was worth seeing.

Suddenly Mrs. Carmody cried in her rusty but powerful old voice, "Don't go out there!"

People turned around to look at her. The orderly shape of the lines had grown fuzzy as people left to get a look at the mist, or as they drew away from Mrs. Carmody, or as they milled around, seeking out their friends. A pretty young woman in a cranberry-colored sweatshirt and dark green slacks was looking at Mrs. Carmody in a thoughtful, evaluating way. A few opportunists were taking advantage of whatever the situation was to move up a couple of places. The checker beside Bud Brown looked over her shoulder again, and Brown tapped her shoulder with a long finger. "Keep your mind on what you're doing, Sally."

"Don't go out there!" Mrs. Carmody yelled. "It's death! I feel that it's death out there!"

Bud and Ollie Weeks, who both knew her, just looked impatient and irritated, but any summer people around her stepped smartly away, never minding their places in line. The bag-ladies in big cities seem to have the same effect on people, as if they were carriers of some contagious disease. Who knows? Maybe they are.

Things began to happen at an accelerating, confusing pace then. A man staggered into the market, shoving the IN door open. His nose was bleeding. "Something in the fog!" he screamed, and Billy shrank against me—whether because of the man's bloody nose or what he was saying, I don't know. "Something in the fog! Something in the fog took John Lee! Something—" He staggered back against a display of lawn food stacked by the window and sat down there. *"Something in the fog took John Lee and I heard him screaming!"*

The situation changed. Made nervous by the storm, by the police siren and the fire whistle, by the subtle dislocation any power outage causes in the American psyche, and by the steadily mounting atmosphere of unease as things somehow . . . somehow *changed* (I don't know how to put it any better than that), people began to move in a body.

They didn't bolt. If I told you that, I would be giving you entirely the wrong impression. It wasn't exactly a panic. They didn't run—or at least, most of them didn't. But they went. Some of them just went to the big show window on the far side of the checkout lanes to look out. Others went out the IN door, some still carrying their intended purchases. Bud Brown, harried and officious, began yelling: "Hey! You haven't paid for that! Hey, you! Come back here with those hot-dog rolls!"

Someone laughed at him, a crazy, yodeling sound that made other people smile. Even as they smiled they looked bewildered, confused, and nervous. Then someone else laughed and Brown flushed. He grabbed a box of mushrooms away from a lady who was crowding past him to look out the window—the segments of glass were lined with people now; they were like the folks you see looking through loopholes into a building site—and the lady screamed, "Give me back my mushies!" This bizarre term of affection caused two men standing nearby to break into crazy laughter—and there was something of the old English Bedlam about all of it, now. Mrs. Carmody trumpeted again not to go out there. The fire whistle whooped breathlessly, a strong old woman who had scared up a prowler in the house. And Billy burst into tears.

"Daddy, what's that bloody man? Why is that bloody man?"

"It's okay, Big Bill, it's his nose, he's okay."

"What did he mean, something in the fog?" Norton asked. He was frowning ponderously, which was probably Norton's way of looking confused.

"Daddy, I'm scared," Billy said through his tears. "Can we please go home?"

Someone bumped past me roughly, jolting me off my feet, and I picked Billy up. I was getting scared, too. The confusion was mounting. Sally, the checker by Bud Brown, started away and he grabbed her back by the collar of her red smock. It ripped. She slap-clawed out at him, her face twisting. *"Get your fucking hands off me!"* she screamed.

"Oh, shut up, you little bitch," Brown said, but he sounded totally astounded.

He reached for her again and Ollie Weeks said sharply: "Bud! Cool it!"

Someone else screamed. It hadn't been a panic before—not quite—but it was getting to be one. People streamed out of both doors. There was a crash of breaking glass and Coke fizzed suddenly across the floor.

"What the Christ *is* this?" Norton exclaimed.

That was when it started getting dark . . . but no, that's not exactly right. My thought at the time was not that it was getting dark but that the lights in the market had gone out. I looked up at the fluorescents in a quick reflex action, and I wasn't alone. And at first, until I remembered the power failure, it seemed that was it, that was what had changed the quality of the light. Then I remembered they had been out all the time we had been in the market and things hadn't seemed dark before. Then I knew, even before the people at the window started to yell and point.

The mist was coming.

It came from the Kansas Road entrance to the parking lot, and even this close it looked no different than it had when we first noticed it on the far side of the lake. It was white and bright but nonreflecting. It was moving fast, and it had blotted out most of the sun. Where the sun had been there was now a silver coin in the sky, like a full moon in winter seen through a thin scud of cloud.

It came with lazy speed. Watching it reminded me somehow of last evening's waterspout. There are big forces in nature that you hardly ever see—earthquakes, hurricanes, tornadoes—I haven't seen them all but I've seen enough to guess that they all move with that lazy, hypnotizing speed. They hold you spellbound, the way Billy and Steffy had been in front of the picture window last night.

It rolled impartially across the two-lane blacktop and erased it from view. The McKeons' nice restored Dutch Colonial was swallowed whole. For a moment the second floor of the ramshackle apartment building next door jutted out of the whiteness, and then it went too. The KEEP RIGHT sign at the entrance and exit points to the Federal's parking lot disappeared, the black letters on the sign seeming to float for a moment in limbo after the sign's dirty white background was gone. The cars in the parking lot began to disappear next.

"What the Christ *is* this?" Norton asked again, and there was a catch in his voice.

It came on, eating up the blue sky and the fresh black hottop with equal ease. Even twenty feet away the line of demarcation was perfectly clear. I had the nutty feeling that I was watching some extra-good piece of visual effects, something dreamed up by Willys O'Brian or Douglas Trumbull. It happened so quickly. The blue sky disappeared to a wide swipe, then to a stripe, then to a pencil line. Then it was gone. Blank white pressed against the glass of the wide show window. I could see as far as the litter barrel that stood maybe four feet away, but not much farther. I could see the front bumper of my Scout, but that was all.

A woman screamed, very loud and long. Billy pressed himself more tightly against me. His body was trembling like a loose bundle of wires with high voltage running through them.

A man yelled and bolted through one of the deserted lanes toward the door. I think that was what finally started the stampede. People rushed pell-mell into the fog.

"Hey!" Brown roared. I don't know if he was angry, scared, or both. His face was nearly purple. Veins stood out on his neck, looking almost as thick as battery cables. *"Hey, you people, you can't take that stuff. Get back here with that stuff, you're shoplifting!"*

They kept going, but some of them tossed their stuff aside. Some were laughing and excited, but they were a minority. They poured out into the fog, and none of us who stayed ever saw them again. There was a faint, acrid smell drifting in through the open door. People began to jam up there. Some pushing and shoving started. I was getting an ache in my shoulders from holding Billy. He was good-sized; Steff sometimes called him her young heifer.

Norton started to wander off, his face preoccupied and rather bemused. He was heading for the door.

I switched Billy to the other arm so I could grab Norton's arm before he drifted out of reach. "No, man, I wouldn't," I said.

He turned back. "What?"

"Better wait and see."

"See what?"

"I don't know," I said.

"You don't think—" he began, and a shriek came out of the fog.

Norton shut up. The tight jam at the OUT door loosened and then reversed itself. The babble of excited conversation, shouts and calls, subsided. The faces of the people by the door suddenly looked flat and pale and two dimensional.

The shriek went on and on, competing with the fire whistle. It seemed impossible that any human pair of lungs could have enough air in them to sustain such a shriek. Norton muttered, "Oh my God," and ran his hands through his hair.

The shriek ended abruptly. It did not dwindle; it was cut off. One more man went outside, a beefy guy in chino workpants. I think he was set on rescuing the shrieker. For a moment he was out there, visible through the glass and the mist, like a figure seen through milk scum on a tumbler. Then (and as far as I know, I was the only one to see this) something beyond him appeared to move, a gray shadow in all that white. And it seemed to me that instead of running into the fog, the man in the chino pants was *jerked* into it, his hands flailing upward as if in surprise.

For a moment there was total silence in the market.

A constellation of moons suddenly glowed into being outside. The parking-lot sodium lights, undoubtedly supplied by underground electrical cables, had just gone on.

"Don't go out there," Mrs. Carmody said in her best gore-crow voice. "It's death to go out there."

All at once, no one seemed disposed to argue or laugh.

Another scream came from outside, this one muffled and rather distant-sounding. Billy tensed against me again.

"David, what's going on?" Ollie Weeks asked. He had left his position. There were big beads of sweat on his round, smooth face. "What is this?"

"I'll be goddamned if I have any idea," I said. Ollie looked badly scared. He was a bachelor who lived in a nice little house up by Highland Lake and who liked to drink in the bar at Pleasant Mountain. On the pudgy little finger of his left hand was a star-sapphire ring. The February before, he won some money in the state lottery. He bought the ring out of his winnings. I always had the idea that Ollie was a little afraid of girls.

"I don't dig this," he said.

"No. Billy, I have to put you down. I'll hold your hand, but you're breaking my arms, okay?"

"Mommy," he whispered.

"She's okay," I told him. It was something to say.

The old geezer who runs the secondhand shop near Jon's Restaurant walked past us, bundled into the old collegiate letter-sweater he wears year-round. He said loudly: "It's one of those pollution clouds. The mills at Rumford and South Paris. Chemicals." With that, he made off up the Aisle 4, past the patent medicines and toilet paper.

"Let's get out of here, David," Norton said with no conviction at all. "What do you say we—"

There was a thud. An odd, twisting thud that I felt mostly in my feet, as if the entire building had suddenly dropped three feet. Several people cried out in fear and surprise. There was a musical jingle of bottles leaning off their shelves and destroying themselves upon the tile floor. A chunk of glass shaped like a pie wedge fell out of one of the segments of the wide front window, and I saw that the wooden frames banding the heavy sections of glass had buckled and splintered in some places.

The fire whistle stopped in midwhoop.

The quiet that followed was the bated silence of people waiting for something else, something more. I was shocked and numb, and my mind made a strange cross-patch connection with the past. Back when Bridgton was little more than a crossroads, my dad would take me in with him and stand talking at the counter while I looked through the glass at the penny candy and two-cent chews. It was January thaw. No sound but the drip of meltwater falling from the galvanized tin gutters to the rain barrels on either side of the store. Me looking at the jawbreakers and buttons and pinwheels. The mystic yellow globes of light overhead showing up the monstrous, projected shadows of last summer's battalion of dead flies. A little boy named David Drayton with his father, the famous artist Andrew Drayton, whose painting *Christine Standing Alone* hung in the White House. A little boy named David Drayton looking at the candy and the Davy Crockett bubblegum cards and vaguely needing to go pee. And outside, the pressing, billowing yellow fog of January thaw.

The memory passed, but very slowly.

"You people!" Norton bellowed. "All you people, listen to me!"

They looked around. Norton was holding up both hands, the fingers splayed like a political candidate accepting accolades.

"It may be dangerous to go outside!" Norton yelled.

"Why?" a woman screamed back. "My kids're at home! I got to get back to my kids!"

"It's death to go out there!" Mrs. Carmody came back smartly. She was standing by the twenty-five-pound sacks of fertilizer stacked below the window, and her face seemed to bulge somehow, as if she were swelling.

A teenager gave her a sudden hard push and she sat down on the bags with a surprised grunt. "Stop saying that, you old bag! Stop rappin' that crazy bullshit!"

"Please!" Norton yelled. "If we just wait a few moments until it blows over and we can see—"

A babble of conflicting shouts greeted this.

"He's right," I said, shouting to be heard over the noise. "Let's just try to keep cool."

"I think that was an earthquake," a bespectacled man said. His voice was soft. In one hand he held a package of hamburger and a bag of buns. The other hand was holding the hand of a little girl, maybe a year younger than Billy. "I really think that was an earthquake."

"They had one over in Naples four years ago," a fat local man said.

"That was in Casco," his wife contradicted immediately. She spoke in the unmistakable tones of a veteran contradictor.

"Naples," the fat local man said, but with less assurance.

"Casco," his wife said firmly, and he gave up.

Somewhere a can that had been jostled to the very edge of its shelf by the thump, earthquake, whatever it had been, fell off with a delayed clatter. Billy burst into tears. "I want to go *home!* I want my MOTHER!"

"Can't you shut that kid up?" Bud Brown asked. His eyes were darting rapidly but aimlessly from place to place.

"Would you like a shot in the teeth, motormouth?" I asked him.

"Come on, Dave, that's not helping," Norton said distractedly.

"I'm sorry," the woman who had screamed earlier said. "I'm sorry, but I can't stay here. I've got to get home and see to my kids."

She looked around at us, a blond woman with a tired, pretty face.

"Wanda's looking after little Victor, you see. Wanda's only eight and sometimes she forgets . . . forgets she's supposed to be . . . well, watching him, you know. And little Victor . . . he likes to turn on the stove burners to see the little red light come on . . .

he likes that light . . . and sometimes he pulls out the plugs . . . little Victor does . . . and Wanda gets . . . bored watching him after a while . . . she's just eight . . ." She stopped talking and just looked at us. I imagine that we must have looked like nothing but a bank of merciless eyes to her right then, not human beings at all, just eyes. *"Isn't anyone going to help me?"* she screamed. Her lips began to tremble. "Won't . . . won't anybody here see a lady home?"

No one replied. People shuffled their feet. She looked from face to face with her own broken face. The fat local man took a hesitant half-step forward and his wife jerked him back with one quick tug, her hand clapped over his wrist like a manacle.

"You?" the blond woman asked Ollie. He shook his head. "You?" she said to Bud. He put his hand over the Texas Instruments calculator on the counter and made no reply. "You?" she said to Norton, and Norton began to say something in his big lawyer's voice, something about how no one should go off half-cocked, and . . . and she dismissed him and Norton just trailed off.

"You?" she said to me, and I picked Billy up again and held him in my arms like a shield to ward off her terrible broken face.

"I hope you all rot in hell," she said. She didn't scream it. Her voice was dead tired. She went to the OUT door and pulled it open, using both hands. I wanted to say something to her, call her back, but my mouth was too dry.

"Aw, lady, listen—" the teenage kid who had

shouted at Mrs. Carmody began. He held her arm. She looked down at his hand and he let her go, shamefaced. She slipped out into the fog. We watched her go and no one said anything. We watched the fog overlay her and make her insubstantial, not a human being anymore but a pencil-ink sketch of a human being done on the world's whitest paper, and no one said anything. For a moment it was like the letters of the KEEP RIGHT sign that had seemed to float on nothingness; her arms and legs and pallid blond hair were all gone and only the misty remnants of her red summer dress remained, seeming to dance in white limbo. Then her dress was gone, too, and no one said anything.

IV

The Storage Area. Problems with the Generators. What Happened to the Bag-Boy.

Billy began to act hysterical and tantrummy, screaming for his mother in a hoarse, demanding way
through his tears, instantly regressing to the age of
two. Snot was lathered on his upper lip. I led him
away, walking down one of the middle aisles with
my arm around his shoulders, trying to soothe him.
I took him back by the long white meat cabinet that
ran the length of the store at the back. Mr. McVey,
the butcher, was still there. We nodded at each other,
the best we could do under the circumstances.

I sat down on the floor and took Billy on my lap
and held his face against my chest and rocked him
and talked to him. I told him all the lies parents keep
in reserve for bad situations, the ones that sound so
damn plausible to a child, and I told them in a tone
of perfect conviction.

"That's not regular fog," Billy said. He looked up
at me, his eyes dark-circled and tear-streaked. "It
isn't, is it, Daddy?"

"No, I don't think so." I didn't want to lie about that.

Kids don't fight shock the way adults do; they go with it, maybe because kids are in a semipermanent state of shock until they're thirteen or so. Billy started to doze off. I held him, thinking he might snap awake again, but his doze deepened into a real sleep. Maybe he had been awake part of the night before, when we had slept three-in-a-bed for the first time since Billy was an infant. And maybe—I felt a cold eddy slip through me at the thought—maybe he had sensed something coming.

When I was sure he was solidly out, I laid him on the floor and went looking for something to cover him up with. Most of the people were still up front, looking out into the thick blanket of mist. Norton had gathered a little crowd of listeners, and was busy spellbinding—or trying to. Bud Brown stood rigidly at his post, but Ollie Weeks had left his.

There were a few people in the aisles, wandering like ghosts, their faces greasy with shock. I went into the storage area through the big double doors between the meat cabinet and the beer cooler.

The generator roared steadily behind its plywood partition, but something had gone wrong. I could smell diesel fumes, and they were much too strong. I walked toward the partition, taking shallow breaths. At last I unbuttoned my shirt and put part of it over my mouth and nose.

The storage area was long and narrow, feebly lit by two sets of emergency lights. Cartons were stacked everywhere—bleach on one side, cases of soft drinks on the far side of the partition, stacked cases of Beefaroni and catsup. One of those had fallen over and the cardboard carton appeared to be bleeding.

I unlatched the door in the generator partition and stepped through. The machine was obscured in drifting, oily clouds of blue smoke. The exhaust pipe ran out through a hole in the wall. Something must have blocked off the outside end of the pipe. There was a simple on/off switch and I flipped it. The generator hitched, belched, coughed, and died. Then it ran down in a diminishing series of popping sounds that reminded me of Norton's stubborn chainsaw.

The emergency lights faded out and I was left in darkness. I got scared very quickly, and I got disoriented. My breathing sounded like a low wind rattling in straw. I bumped my nose on the flimsy plywood door going out and my heart lurched. There were windows in the double doors, but for some reason they had been painted black, and the darkness was nearly total. I got off course and ran into a stack of the bleach cartons. They tumbled and fell. One came close enough to my head to make me step backward, and I tripped over another carton that had landed behind me. I fell down, thumping my head hard enough to see bright stars in the darkness. Good show.

I lay there cursing myself and rubbing my head, telling myself to just take it easy, just get up and get out of here, get back to Billy, telling myself nothing soft and slimy was going to close over my ankle or slip into one groping hand. I told myself not to lose control, or I would end up blundering around back here in a panic, knocking things over and creating a mad obstacle course for myself.

I stood up carefully, looking for a pencil line of light between the double doors. I found it, a faint but unmistakable scratch on the darkness. I started toward it, and then stopped.

There was a sound. A soft sliding sound. It stopped, then started again with a stealthy little bump. Everything inside me went loose. I regressed magically to four years of age. That sound wasn't coming from the market. It was coming from behind me. From outside. Where the mist was. Something that was slipping and sliding and scraping over the cinderblocks. And, maybe, looking for a way in.

Or maybe it was already in, and it was looking for me. Maybe in a moment I would feel whatever was making that sound on my shoe. Or on my neck.

It came again. I was positive it was outside. But that didn't make it any better. I told my legs to go and they refused the order. Then the quality of the noise changed. Something *rasped* across the darkness and my heart leaped in my chest and I lunged at that thin vertical line of light. I hit the doors straight-arm and burst through into the market.

Three or four people were right outside the double doors—Ollie Weeks was one of them—and they all jumped back in surprise. Ollie grabbed at his chest. "David!" he said in a pinched voice. "Jesus Christ, you want to take ten years off my—" He saw my face. "What's the matter with you?"

"Did you hear it?" I asked. My voice sounded strange in my own ears, high and squeaking. "Did any of you hear it?"

They hadn't heard anything, of course. They had come up to see why the generator had gone off. As Ollie told me that, one of the bag-boys bustled up with an armload of flashlights. He looked from Ollie to me curiously.

"I turned the generator off," I said, and explained why.

"What did you hear?" one of the other men asked. He worked for the town road department; his name was Jim something.

"I don't know. A scraping noise. Slithery. I don't want to hear it again."

"Nerves," the other fellow with Ollie said.

No. It was not nerves.

"Did you hear it before the lights went out?"

"No, only after. But . . ." But nothing. I could see the way they were looking at me. They didn't want any more bad news, anything else frightening or off-kilter. There was enough of that already. Only Ollie looked as if he believed me.

"Let's go in and start her up again," the bag-boy said, handing out the flashlights. Ollie took his doubtfully. The bag-boy offered me one, a slightly contemptuous shine in his eyes. He was maybe eighteen. After a moment's thought, I took the light. I still needed something to cover Billy with.

Ollie opened the doors and chocked them, letting in some light. The bleach cartons lay scattered around the half-open door in the plywood partition.

The fellow named Jim sniffed and said, "Smells pretty rank, all right. Guess you was right to shut her down."

The flashlight beams bobbed and danced across cartons of canned goods, toilet paper, dog food. The beams were smoky in the drifting fumes the blocked exhaust had turned back into the storage area. The bag-boy trained his light briefly on the wide loading door at the extreme right.

The two men and Ollie went inside the generator compartment. Their lights flashed uneasily back and forth, reminding me of something out of a boys' adventure story—and I illustrated a series of them while I was still in college. Pirates burying their bloody gold at midnight, or maybe the mad doctor and his assistant snatching a body. Shadows, made twisted and monstrous by the shifting, conflicting flashlight beams, bobbed on the walls. The generator ticked irregularly as it cooled.

The bag-boy was walking toward the loading door, flashing his light ahead of him. "I wouldn't go over there," I said.

"No, I know *you* wouldn't."

"Try it now, Ollie," one of the men said. The generator wheezed, then roared.

"Jesus! Shut her down! Holy crow, don't that *stink!*"

The generator died again.

The bag-boy walked back from the loading door just as they came out. "Something's plugged that exhaust, all right," one of the men said.

"I'll tell you what," the bag-boy said. His eyes were shining in the glow of the flashlights, and there was a devil-may-care expression on his face that I had sketched too many times as part of the frontispieces for my boys' adventure series. "Get it running long enough for me to raise the loading door back there. I'll go around and clear away whatever it is."

"Norm, I don't think that's a very good idea," Ollie said doubtfully.

"Is it an electric door?" the one called Jim asked.

"Sure," Ollie said. "But I just don't think it would be wise for—"

"That's okay," the other guy said. He tipped his baseball cap back on his head. "I'll do it."

"No, you don't understand," Ollie began again. "I really don't think anyone should—"

"Don't worry," he said indulgently to Ollie, dismissing him.

Norm, the bag-boy, was indignant. "Listen, it was my idea," he said.

All at once, by some magic, they had gotten around to arguing about who was going to do it instead of whether or not it should be done at all. But of course, none of them had heard that nasty slithering sound. "Stop it!" I said loudly.

They looked around at me.

"You don't seem to understand, or you're trying as hard as you can *not* to understand. This is no ordinary fog. Nobody has come into the market since it hit. If you open that loading door and something comes in—"

"Something like what?" Norm said with perfect eighteen-year-old macho contempt.

"Whatever made the noise I heard."

"Mr. Drayton," Jim said. "Pardon me, but I'm not convinced you heard anything. I know you're a big-shot artist with connections in New York and Hollywood and all, but that doesn't make you any different from anyone else, in my book. Way I figure, you got in here in the dark and maybe you just . . . got a little confused."

"Maybe I did," I said. "And maybe if you want to start screwing around outside, you ought to start by making sure that lady got home safe to her kids." His attitude—and that of his buddy and of Norm the bag-boy—was making me mad and scaring me more at the same time. They had the sort of light in their eyes that some men get when they go shooting rats at the town dump.

"Hey," Jim's buddy said. "When any of us here want your advice, we'll ask for it."

Hesitantly, Ollie said: "The generator really isn't that important, you know. The food in the cold cases will keep for twelve hours or more with absolutely no—"

"Okay, kid, you're it," Jim said brusquely. "I'll start the motor, you raise the door so that the place doesn't stink up too bad. Me and Myron will be standing by the exhaust outflow. Give us a yell when it's clear."

"Sure," Norm said, and bustled excitedly away.

"This is crazy," I said. "You let that lady go by herself—"

"I didn't notice you breaking your ass to escort her," Jim's buddy Myron said. A dull, brick-colored flush was creeping out of his collar.

"—but you're going to let this kid risk his life over a generator that doesn't even matter?"

"Why don't you just shut the fuck up!" Norm yelled.

"Listen, Mr. Drayton," Jim said, and smiled at me coldly. "I'll tell you what. If you've got anything else to say, I think you better count your teeth first, because I'm tired of listening to your bullshit."

Ollie looked at me, plainly frightened. I shrugged. They were crazy, that was all. Their sense of proportion was temporarily gone. Out there they had been confused and scared. In here was a straightforward mechanical problem: a balky generator. It was possible to solve this problem. Solving the problem would help make them feel less confused and helpless. Therefore they would solve it.

Jim and his friend Myron decided I knew when I was licked and went back into the generator compartment. "Ready, Norm?" Jim asked.

Norm nodded, then realized they couldn't hear a nod. "Yeah," he said.

"Norm," I said. "Don't be a fool."

"It's a mistake," Ollie added.

He looked at us, and suddenly his face was much younger than eighteen. It was the face of a boy. His Adam's apple bobbed convulsively, and I saw that he was scared green. He opened his mouth to say something—I think he was going to call it off—and then the generator roared into life again, and when it was running smoothly, Norm lunged at the button to the right of the door and it began to rattle upward on its dual steel tracks. The emergency lights had come back on when the generator started. Now they dimmed down as the motor which lifted the door sucked away the juice.

The shadows ran backward and melted. The storage area began to fill with the mellow white light of an overcast late-winter day. I noticed that odd, acrid smell again.

The loading door went up two feet, then four. Beyond I could see a square cement platform outlined around the edges with a yellow stripe. The yellow faded and washed out in just three feet. The fog was incredibly thick.

"Ho up!" Norm yelled.

Tendrils of mist, as white and fine as floating lace, eddied inside. The air was cold. It had been noticeably cool all morning long, especially after the sticky heat of the last three weeks, but it had been a summery coolness. This was *cold.* It was like March. I shivered. And I thought of Steff.

The generator died. Jim came out just as Norm

ducked under the door. He saw it. So did I. So did Ollie.

A tentacle came over the far lip of the concrete loading platform and grabbed Norm around the calf. My mouth dropped wide open. Ollie made a very short glottal sound of surprise—*uk!* The tentacle tapered from a thickness of a foot—the size of a grass snake—at the point where it had wrapped itself around Norm's lower leg to a thickness of maybe four or five feet where it disappeared into the mist. It was slate gray on top, shading to a fleshy pink underneath. And there were rows of suckers on the underside. They were moving and writhing like hundreds of small, puckering mouths.

Norm looked down. He saw what had him. His eyes bulged. *"Get it off me! Hey, get it off me! Christ Jesus, get this frigging thing off me!"*

"Oh my God," Jim whimpered.

Norm grabbed the bottom edge of the loading door and yanked himself back in. The tentacle seemed to bulge, the way your arm will when you flex it. Norm was yanked back against the corrugated steel door—his head clanged against it. The tentacle bulged more, and Norm's legs and torso began to slip back out. The bottom edge of the loading door scraped the shirttail out of his pants. He yanked savagely and pulled himself back in like a man doing a chin-up.

"Help me," he was sobbing. "Help me, you guys, please, please."

"Jesus, Mary, and Joseph," Myron said. He had

come out of the generator compartment to see what
was going on.

I was the closest, and I grabbed Norm around the
waist and yanked as hard as I could, rocking back
on my heels. For a moment we moved backward,
but only for a moment. It was like stretching a rubber
band or pulling taffy. The tentacle yielded but gave
up its basic grip not at all. Then three more tentacles
floated out of the mist toward us. One curled around
Norm's flapping red Federal apron and tore it away.
It disappeared back into the mist with the red cloth
curled in its grip and I thought of something my
mother used to say when my brother and I would
beg for something she didn't want us to have—
candy, a comic book, some toy. "You need that like
a hen needs a flag," she'd say. I thought of that, and
I thought of that tentacle waving Norm's red apron
around, and I got laughing. I got laughing, except
my laughter and Norm's screams sounded about the
same. Maybe no one even knew I was laughing except me.

The other two tentacles slithered aimlessly back
and forth on the loading platform for a moment,
making those low scraping sounds I had heard earlier. Then one of them slapped against Norm's left
hip and slipped around it. I felt it touch my arm. It
was warm and pulsing and smooth. I think now that
if it had gripped me with those suckers, I would have
gone out into the mist too. But it didn't. It grabbed
Norm. And the third tentacle ringleted his other
ankle.

Now he was being pulled away from me. "Help me!" I shouted. "Ollie! Someone! Give me a hand here!"

But they didn't come. I don't know what they were doing, but they didn't come.

I looked down and saw the tentacle around Norm's waist working into his skin. The suckers were *eating* him where his shirt had pulled out of his pants. Blood, as red as his missing apron, began to seep out of the trench the pulsing tentacle had made for itself.

I banged my head on the lower edge of the partly raised door.

Norm's legs were outside again. One of his loafers had fallen off. A new tentacle came out of the mist, wrapped its tip firmly around the shoe, and made off with it. Norm's fingers clutched at the door's lower edge. He had it in a death grip. His fingers were livid. He was not screaming anymore; he was beyond that. His head whipped back and forth in an endless gesture of negation, and his long black hair flew wildly.

I looked over his shoulder and saw more tentacles coming, dozens of them, a forest of them. Most were small but a few were gigantic, as thick as the moss-corseted tree that had been lying across our driveway that morning. The big ones had candy pink suckers that seemed the size of manhole covers. One of these big ones struck the concrete loading platform with a loud and rolling *thrrrrap!* sound and moved slug-gishly toward us like a great blind earthworm. I gave one gigantic tug, and the tentacle holding Norm's right calf slipped a little. That was all. But before it reestablished its grip, I saw that the thing was eating him away.

One of the tentacles brushed delicately past my cheek and then wavered in the air, as if debating. I thought of Billy then. Billy was lying asleep in the market by Mr. McVey's long white meat cooler. I had come in here to find something to cover him up with. If one of those things got hold of me, there would be no one to watch out for him—except maybe Norton.

So I let go of Norm and dropped to my hands and knees.

I was half in and half out, directly under the raised door. A tentacle passed by on my left, seeming to walk on its suckers. It attached itself to one of Norm's bulging upper arms, paused for a second, and then slid around it in coils.

Now Norm looked like something out of a madman's dream of snake charming. Tentacles twisted over him uneasily almost everywhere . . . and they were all around me, as well. I made a clumsy leap-frog jump back inside, landed on my shoulder, and rolled. Jim, Ollie and Myron were still there. They stood like a tableau of waxworks in Madame Tussaud's, their faces pale, their eyes too bright. Jim and Myron flanked the door to the generator compartment.

"Start the generator!" I yelled at them.

Neither moved. They were staring with a drugged, thanatotic avidity at the loading bay.

I groped on the floor, picked up the first thing that came to hand—a box of Snowy bleach—and chucked it at Jim. It hit him in the gut, just above the belt buckle. He grunted and grabbed at himself. His eyes flickered back into some semblance of normality.

"Go start that fucking generator!" I screamed so loudly it hurt my throat.

He didn't move; instead he began to defend himself, apparently having decided that, with Norm being eaten alive by some insane horror from the mist, the time had come for rebuttals.

"I'm sorry," he whined. "I didn't know, how the hell was I supposed to know? You said you heard something but I didn't know what you meant, you should have said what you meant better. I thought, I dunno, maybe a bird, or something—"

So then Ollie moved, bunting him aside with one thick shoulder and blundering into the generator room. Jim stumbled over one of the bleach cartons and fell down, just as I had done in the dark. "I'm sorry," he said again. His red hair had tumbled over his brow. His cheeks were cheese white. His eyes were those of a horrified little boy. Seconds later the generator coughed and rumbled into life.

I turned back to the loading door. Norm was almost gone, yet he clung grimly with one hand. His body boiled with tentacles, and blood pattered serenely down on the concrete in dime-size droplets. His head whipped back and forth and his eyes bulged with terror as they stared off into the mist.

Other tentacles now crept and crawled over the

floor inside. There were too many near the button that controlled the loading door to even think of approaching it. One of them closed around a half-liter bottle of Pepsi and carried it off. Another slipped around a cardboard carton and squeezed. The carton ruptured and rolls of toilet paper, two-packs of Delsey wrapped in cellophane, geysered upward, came down, and rolled everywhere. Tentacles seized them eagerly.

One of the big ones slipped in. Its tip rose from the floor and it seemed to sniff the air. It began to advance toward Myron and he stepped mincingly away from it, his eyes rolling madly in their sockets. A high-pitched little moan escaped his slack lips.

I looked around for something, anything at all long enough to reach over the questing tentacles and punch the SHUT button on the wall. I saw a janitor's push broom leaning against a stack-up of beer cases and grabbed it.

Norm's good hand was ripped loose. He thudded down onto the concrete loading platform and scrabbled madly for a grip with his one free hand. His eyes met mine for a moment. They were hellishly bright and aware. He knew what was happening to him. Then he was pulled, bumping and rolling, into the mist. There was another scream, choked off. Norm was gone.

I pushed the tip of the broom handle onto the button and the motor whined. The door began to slide back down. It touched the thickest of the tentacles first, the one that had been investigating in Myron's direction. It indented its hide—skin, whatever—and then pierced it. A black goo began to spurt from it. It writhed madly, whipping across the concrete storage-area floor like an obscene bullwhip, and then it seemed to flatten out. A moment later it was gone. The others began to withdraw.

One of them had a five-pound bag of Gaines dog food, and it wouldn't let go. The descending door cut it in two before thumping home in its grooved slot. The severed chunk of tentacle squeezed convulsively tighter, splitting the bag open and sending brown nuggets of dog food everywhere. Then it began to flop on the floor like a fish out of water, curling and uncurling, but ever more slowly, until it lay still. I prodded it with the tip of the broom. The piece of tentacle, maybe three feet long, closed on it savagely for a moment, then loosened and lay limp again in the confused litter of toilet paper, dog food, and bleach cartons.

There was no sound except the roar of the generator and Ollie, crying inside the plywood compartment. I could see him sitting on a stool in there with his face clutched in his hands.

Then I became aware of another sound. The soft, slithery sound I had heard in the dark. Only now the sound was multiplied tenfold. It was the sound of tentacles squirming over the outside of the loading door, trying to find a way in.

Myron took a couple of steps toward me. "Look," he said. "You got to understand—"

I looped a fist at his face. He was too surprised to

even try to block it. It landed just below his nose and mashed his upper lip into his teeth. Blood flowed into his mouth.

"You got him killed!" I shouted. "Did you get a good look at it? Did you get a good look at what you did?"

I started to pummel him, throwing wild rights and lefts, not punching the way I had been taught in my college boxing classes but only hitting out. He stepped back, shaking some of them off, taking others with a numbness that seemed like a kind of resignation or penance. That made me angrier. I bloodied his nose. I raised a mouse under one of his eyes that was going to black just beautifully. I clipped him a hard one on the chin. After that one, his eyes went cloudy and semi-vacant.

"Look," he kept saying, "look, look," and then I punched him low in the stomach and the air went out of him and he didn't say "look, look" anymore. I don't know how long I would have gone on punching him, but someone grabbed my arms. I jerked free and turned around. I was hoping it was Jim. I wanted to punch Jim out, too.

But it wasn't Jim. It was Ollie, his round face dead pale, except for the dark circles around his eyes—eyes that were still shiny from his tears. "Don't, David," he said. "Don't hit him anymore. It doesn't solve anything."

Jim was standing off to one side, his face a bewildered blank. I kicked a carton of something at him. It struck one of his Dingo boots and bounced away.

"You and your buddy are a couple of stupid assholes," I said.

"Come on, David," Ollie said unhappily. "Quit it."

"You two assholes got that kid killed."

Jim looked down at his Dingo boots. Myron sat on the floor and held his beer belly. I was breathing hard. The blood was roaring in my ears and I was trembling all over. I sat down on a couple of cartons and put my head down between my knees and gripped my legs hard just above the ankles. I sat that way for a while with my hair in my face, waiting to see if I was going to black out or puke or what.

After a bit the feeling began to pass and I looked up at Ollie. His pinky ring flashed subdued fire in the glow of the emergency lights.

"Okay," I said dully. "I'm done."

"Good," Ollie said. "We've got to think what to do next."

The storage area was beginning to stink of exhaust again. "Shut the generator down. That's the first thing."

"Yeah, let's get out of here," Myron said. His eyes appealed to me. "I'm sorry about the kid. But you got to understand—"

"I don't got to understand anything. You and your buddy go back into the market, but you wait right there by the beer cooler. And don't say a word to anybody. Not yet."

They went willingly enough, huddling together as they passed through the swinging doors. Ollie killed the generator, and just as the lights started to fail, I saw a quilted rug—the sort of thing movers use to pad breakable things—flopped over a stack of returnable soda bottles. I reached up and grabbed it for Billy.

There was the shuffling, blundering sound of Ollie coming out of the generator compartment. Like a great many overweight men, his breathing had a slightly heavy wheezing sound.

"David?" His voice wavered a little. "You still here?"

"Right here, Ollie. You want to watch out for all those bleach cartons."

"Yeah."

I guided him with my voice and in thirty seconds or so he reached out of the dark and gripped my shoulder. He gave a long, trembling sigh.

"Christ, let's get out of here." I could smell the Rolaids he always chewed on his breath. "This dark is . . . is bad."

"It is," I said. "But hang tight a minute, Ollie. I wanted to talk to you and I didn't want those other two fuckheads listening."

"Dave . . . they didn't twist Norm's arm. You ought to remember that."

"Norm was a kid, and they weren't. But never mind, that's over. We've got to tell them, Ollie. The people in the market."

"If they panic—" Ollie's voice was doubtful.

"Maybe they will and maybe they won't. But it will make them think twice about going out, which is what most of them want to do. Why shouldn't they? Most of them will have people they left at home. I do myself. We have to make them understand what they're risking if they go out there."

His hand was gripping my arm hard. "All right," he said. "Yes, I just keep asking myself . . . all those tentacles . . . like a squid or something . . . David, what were they hooked to? *What were those tentacles hooked to?*"

"I don't know. But I don't want those two telling people on their own. That *would* start a panic. Let's go."

I looked around, and after a moment or two located the thin line of vertical light between the swing doors. We started to shuffle toward it, wary of scattered cartons, one of Ollie's pudgy hands clamped over my forearm. It occurred to me that all of us had lost our flashlights.

As we reached the doors, Ollie said flatly: "What we saw . . . it's impossible, David. You know that, don't you? Even if a van from the Boston Seaquarium drove out back and dumped out one of those gigantic squids like in *Twenty Thousand Leagues Under the Sea*, it would die. *It would just die.*"

"Yes," I said. "That's right."

"So what happened? Huh? What happened? What is that damned mist?"

"Ollie, I don't know."

We went out.

V

An Argument with Norton.
A Discussion Near
the Beer Cooler.
Verification.

Jim and his good buddy Myron were just outside the doors, each with a Budweiser in his fist. I looked at Billy, saw he was still asleep, and covered him with the ruglike mover's pad. He moved a little, muttered something, and then lay still again. I looked at my watch. It was 12:15 P.M. That seemed utterly impossible; it felt as if at least five hours had passed since I had first gone in there to look for something to cover him with. But the whole thing, from first to last, had taken only about thirty-five minutes.

I went back to where Ollie stood with Jim and Myron. Ollie had taken a beer and he offered me one. I took it and gulped down half the can at once, as I had that morning cutting wood. It bucked me up a little.

Jim was Jim Grondin. Myron's last name was LaFleur—that had its comic side, all right. Myron the flower had drying blood on his lips, chin, and cheek. The eye with the mouse under it was already swelling up. The girl in the cranberry-colored sweatshirt walked by aimlessly and gave Myron a cautious look. I could have told her that Myron was only dangerous to teenage boys intent on proving their manhood, but saved my breath. After all, Ollie was right—they *had* only been doing what they thought was best, although in a blind, fearful way rather than in any real common interest. And now I needed them to do what *I* thought was best. I didn't think that would be a problem. They had both had the stuffing knocked out of them. Neither—especially Myron the flower—was going to be good for anything for some time to come. Something that had been in their eyes when they were fixing to send Norm out to unplug the exhaust vent had gone now. Their peckers were no longer up.

"We're going to have to tell these people something," I said.

Jim opened his mouth to protest.

"Ollie and I will leave out any part you and Myron had in sending Norm out there if you'll back up what he and I say about . . . well, about what got him."

"Sure," Jim said, pitifully eager. "Sure, if we don't tell, people might go out there . . . like that woman . . . that woman who . . ." He wiped his hand across his mouth and then drank more beer quickly. "Christ, what a mess."

"David," Ollie said. "What—" He stopped, then made himself go on. "What if they get in? The tentacles?"

"How could they?" Jim asked. "You guys shut the door."

"Sure," Ollie said. "But the whole front wall of this place is plate glass."

An elevator shot my stomach down about twenty floors. I had known that, but had somehow been successfully ignoring it. I looked over at where Billy lay asleep. I thought of those tentacles swarming over Norm. I thought about that happening to Billy.

"Plate glass," Myron LaFleur whispered. "Jesus Christ in a chariot-driven sidecar."

I left the three of them standing by the cooler, each working a second can of beer, and went looking for Brent Norton. I found him in sober-sided conversation with Bud Brown at Register 2. The pair of them—Norton with his styled gray hair and his elderly-stud good looks, Brown with his dour New England phiz—looked like something out of a *New Yorker* cartoon.

As many as two dozen people milled restlessly in the space between the end of the checkout lanes and the long show window. A lot of them were lined up at the glass, looking out into the mist. I was again reminded of the people that congregate at a building site.

Mrs. Carmody was seated on the stationary conveyor belt of one of the checkout lanes, smoking a Parliament in a One Step at a Time filter. Her eyes measured me, found me wanting, and passed on. She looked as if she might be dreaming awake.

"Brent," I said.

"David! Where did you get off to?"

"That's what I'd like to talk to you about."

"There are people back at the cooler drinking beer," Brown said grimly. He sounded like a man announcing that X-rated movies had been shown at the deacons' party. "I can see them in the security mirror. This has simply got to stop."

"Brent?"

"Excuse me for a minute, would you, Mr. Brown?"

"Certainly." He folded his arms across his chest and stared grimly up into the convex mirror. "It *is* going to stop, I can promise you that."

Norton and I headed toward the beer cooler in the far corner of the store, walking past the housewares and notions. I glanced back over my shoulder, noticing uneasily how the wooden beams framing the tall, rectangular sections of glass had buckled and twisted and splintered. And one of the windows wasn't even whole, I remembered. A pie-shaped chunk of glass had fallen out of the upper corner at the instant of that queer thump. Perhaps we could stuff it with cloth or something—maybe a bunch of those $3.59 ladies' tops I had noticed near the wine—

My thoughts broke off abruptly, and I had to put the back of my hand over my mouth, as if stifling a burp. What I was really stifling was the rancid flood of horrified giggles that wanted to escape me at the thought of stuffing a bunch of shirts into a hole to keep out those tentacles that had carried Norm away.

I had seen one of those tentacles—a small one—squeeze a bag of dog food until it simply ruptured.

"David? Are you okay?"

"Huh?"

"Your face—you looked like you just had a good idea or a bloody awful one."

Something hit me then. "Brent, what happened to that man who came in raving about something in the mist getting John Lee Frovin?"

"The guy with the nosebleed?"

"Yes, him."

"He passed out and Mr. Brown brought him around with some smelling salts from the first-aid kit. Why?"

"Did he say anything else when he woke up?"

"He started in on that hallucination. Mr. Brown conducted him up to the office. He was frightening some of the women. He seemed happy enough to go. Something about the glass. When Mr. Brown said there was only one small window in the manager's office, and that that one was reinforced with wire, he seemed happy enough to go. I presume he's still there."

"What he was talking about is no hallucination."

"No, of course it isn't."

"And that thud we felt?"

"No, but, David—"

He's scared, I kept reminding myself. Don't blow up at him, you've treated yourself to one blowup this morning and that's enough. Don't blow up at him just because this is the way he was during that stupid property-line dispute . . . first patronizing, then sarcastic, and finally, when it became clear he was going to lose, ugly. Don't blow up at him because you're going to need him. He may not be able to start his own chainsaw, but he looks like the father figure of the Western world, and if he tells people not to panic, they won't. So don't blow up at him.

"You see those double doors up there beyond the beer cooler?"

He looked, frowning. "Isn't one of those men drinking beer the other assistant manager? Weeks? If Brown sees that, I can promise you that man will be looking for a job very soon."

"Brent, will you listen to me?"

He glanced back at me absently. "What were you saying, Dave? I'm sorry."

Not as sorry as he was going to be. "Do you see those doors?"

"Yes, of course I do. What about them?"

"They give on the storage area that runs all the way along the west face of the building. Billy fell asleep and I went back there to see if I could find something to cover him up with . . ."

I told him everything, only leaving out the argument about whether or not Norm should have gone out at all. I told him what had come in . . . and finally, what had gone out, screaming. Brent Norton refused to believe it. No—he refused to even entertain it. I took him over to Jim, Ollie, and Myron. All three of them verified the story, although Jim and

Myron the flower were well on their way to getting drunk.

Again, Norton refused to believe or even to entertain it. He simply balked. "No," he said. "No, no, no. Forgive me, gentlemen, but it's completely ridiculous. Either you're having me on"—he patronized us with his gleaming smile to show that he could take a joke as well as the next fellow—"or you're suffering from some form of group hypnosis."

My temper rose again, and I controlled it—with difficulty. I don't think that I'm ordinarily a quick-tempered man, but these weren't ordinary circumstances. I had Billy to think about, and what was happening—or what had already happened—to Stephanie. Those things were constantly gnawing at the back of my mind.

"All right," I said. "Let's go back there. There's a chunk of tentacle on the floor. The door cut it off when it came down. And you can *hear* them. They're rustling all over that door. It sounds like the wind in ivy."

"No," he said calmly.

"What?" I really did believe I had misheard him. "What did you say?"

"I said no, I'm not going back there. The joke has gone far enough."

"Brent, I swear to you it's no joke."

"Of course it is," he snapped. His eyes ran over Jim, Myron, rested briefly on Ollie Weeks—who held his glance with calm impassivity—and at last came back to me. "It's what you locals probably call 'a real belly-buster.' Right, David?"

"Brent . . . look—"

"No, you look!" His voice began to rise toward a courtroom shout. It carried very, very well, and several of the people who were wandering around, edgy and aimless, looked over to see what was going on. Norton jabbed his finger at me as he spoke. "It's a joke. It's a banana skin and I'm the guy that's supposed to slip on it. None of you people are exactly crazy about out-of-towners, am I right? You all pretty much stick together. The way it happened when I hauled you into court to get what was rightfully mine. You won that one, all right. Why not? Your father was the famous artist, and it's your town. I only pay my taxes and spend my money here!"

He was no longer performing, hectoring us with the trained courtroom shout; he was nearly screaming and on the verge of losing all control. Ollie Weeks turned and walked away, clutching his beer. Myron and his friend Jim were staring at Norton with frank amazement.

"Am I supposed to go back there and look at some ninety-eight-cent rubber-joke novelty while these two hicks stand around and laugh their asses off?"

"Hey, you want to watch who you're calling a hick," Myron said.

"I'm *glad* that tree fell on your boathouse, if you want to know the truth. *Glad.*" Norton was grinning savagely at me. "Stove it in pretty well, didn't it? Fantastic. Now get out of my way."

He tried to push past me. I grabbed him by the

arm and threw him against the beer cooler. A woman cawed in surprise. Two six-packs of Bud fell over.

"You dig out your ears and listen, Brent. There are lives at stake here. My kid's is not the least of them. So you listen, or I swear I'll knock the shit out of you."

"Go ahead," Norton said, still grinning with a kind of insane palsied bravado. His eyes, bloodshot and wide, bulged from their sockets. "Show everyone how big and brave you are, beating up a man with a heart condition who is old enough to be your father."

"Sock him anyway!" Jim exclaimed. "Fuck his heart condition. I don't even think a cheap New York shyster like him has got a heart."

"You keep out of it," I said to Jim, and then put my face down to Norton's. I was kissing distance, if that had been what I had in mind. The cooler was off, but it was still radiating a chill. "Stop throwing up sand. You know damn well I'm telling the truth."

"I know . . . no . . . such thing," he panted.

"If it was another time and place, I'd let you get away with it. I don't care how scared you are, and I'm not keeping score. I'm scared, too. But I need you, goddammit! Does that get through? I need you!"

"Let me *go!*"

I grabbed him by the shirt and shook him. "Don't you understand anything? People are going to start leaving and walk right into that thing out there! For Christ's sake, don't you understand?"

"*Let me go!*"

"Not until you come back there with me and see for yourself."

"I told you, *no!* It's all a trick, a joke. I'm not as stupid as you take me for—"

"Then I'll haul you back there myself."

I grabbed him by the shoulder and the scruff of his neck. The seam of his shirt under one arm tore with a soft purring sound. I dragged him toward the double doors. Norton let out a wretched scream. A knot of people, fifteen or eighteen, had gathered, but they kept their distance. None showed any signs of wanting to interfere.

"Help me!" Norton cried. His eyes bulged behind his glasses. His styled hair had gone awry again, sticking up in the same two little tufts behind his ears. People shuffled their feet and watched.

"What are you screaming for?" I said in his ear. "It's just a joke, right? That's why I took you to town when you asked to come and why I trusted you to cross Billy in the parking lot—because I had this handy fog all manufactured, I rented a fog machine from Hollywood, it cost me fifteen thousand dollars and another eight thousand dollars to ship it, all so I could play a joke on you. Stop bullshitting yourself and open your eyes!"

"*Let . . . me . . . go!*" Norton bawled. We were almost at the doors.

"Here, here! What is this? What are you doing?"

It was Brown. He bustled and elbowed his way through the crowd of watchers.

"Make him let me go," Norton said hoarsely. "He's crazy."

"No. He's not crazy. I wish he were, but he isn't." That was Ollie, and I could have blessed him. He came around the aisle behind us and stood there facing Brown.

Brown's eyes dropped to the beer Ollie was holding. "You're *drinking!*" he said, and his voice was surprised but not totally devoid of pleasure. "You'll lose your job for this."

"Come on, Bud," I said, letting Norton go. "This is no ordinary situation."

"Regulations don't change," Brown said smugly. "I'll see that the company hears of it. That's my responsibility."

Norton, meanwhile, had skittered away and stood at some distance, trying to straighten his shirt and smooth back his hair. His eyes darted between Brown and me nervously.

"Hey!" Ollie cried suddenly, raising his voice and producing a bass thunder I never would have suspected from this large but soft and unassuming man. *"Hey! Everybody in the store! You want to come up back and hear this! It concerns all of you!"* He looked at me levelly, ignoring Brown altogether. "Am I doing all right?"

"Fine."

People began to gather. The original knot of spectators to my argument with Norton doubled, then trebled.

"There's something you all had better know—" Ollie began.

"You put that beer down right now," Brown said.

"You shut up right now," I said, and took a step toward him.

Brown took a compensatory step back. "I don't know what some of you think you are doing," he said, "but I can tell you it's going to be reported to the Federal Foods Company! All of it! And I want you to understand—*there may be charges!*" His lips drew nervously back from his yellowed teeth, and I could feel sympathy for him. Just trying to cope; that was all he was doing. As Norton was by imposing a mental gag order on himself. Myron and Jim had tried by turning the whole thing into a macho charade—if the generator could be fixed, the mist would blow over. This was Brown's way. He was . . . Protecting the Store.

"Then you go ahead and take down the names," I said. "But please don't talk."

"I'll take down plenty of names," he responded. "Yours will be head on the list, you . . . you *bohemian.*"

"Mr. David Drayton has got something to tell you," Ollie said, "and I think you had better all listen up, in case you were planning on going home."

So I told them what had happened, pretty much as I told Norton. There was some laughter at first, then a deepening uneasiness as I finished.

"It's a lie, you know," Norton said. His voice tried for hard emphasis and overshot into stridency. This was the man I'd told first, hoping to enlist his credibility. What a balls-up.

"Of course it's a lie," Brown agreed. "It's lunacy. Where do you suppose those tentacles came from, Mr. Drayton?"

"I don't know, and at this point, that's not even a very important question. They're here. There's—"

"I suspect they came out of a few of those beer cans. That's what I suspect." This got some appreciative laughter. It was silenced by the strong, rusty-hinge voice of Mrs. Carmody.

"Death!" she cried, and those who had been laughing quickly sobered.

She marched into the center of the rough circle that had formed, her canary pants seeming to give off a light of their own, her huge purse swinging against one elephantine thigh. Her black eyes glanced arrogantly around, as sharp and balefully sparkling as a magpie's. Two good-looking girls of about sixteen with CAMP WOODLANDS written on the back of their white rayon shirts shrank away from her.

"You listen but you don't hear! You hear but you don't believe! Which one of you wants to go outside and see for himself?" Her eyes swept them, and then fell on me. "And just what do you propose to do about it, Mr. David Drayton? What do you think you can do about it?"

She grinned, skull-like above her canary outfit.

"It's the end, I tell you. The end of everything. It's the Last Times. The moving finger has writ, not in fire, but in lines of mist. The earth has opened and spewed forth its abominations—"

"Can't you make her shut up?" one of the teenage

girls burst out. She was beginning to cry. "She's scaring me!"

"Are you scared, dearie?" Mrs. Carmody asked, and turned on her. "You aren't scared now, no. But when the foul creatures the Imp has loosed upon the face of the earth come for you—"

"That's enough now, Mrs. Carmody," Ollie said, taking her arm. "That's just fine."

"You let go of me! It's the end, I tell you! It's death! Death!"

"It's a pile of shit," a man in a fishing hat and glasses said disgustedly.

"No, sir," Myron spoke up. "I know it sounds like something out of a dope-dream, but it's the flat-out truth. I saw it myself."

"I did, too," Jim said.

"And me," Ollie chipped in. He had succeeded in quieting Mrs. Carmody, at least for the time being. But she stood close by, clutching her big purse and grinning her crazy grin. No one wanted to stand too close to her—they muttered among themselves, not liking the corroboration. Several of them looked back at the big plate-glass windows in an uneasy, speculative way. I was glad to see it.

"Lies," Norton said. "You people all lie each other up. That's all."

"What you're suggesting is totally beyond belief," Brown said.

"We don't have to stand here chewing it over," I told him. "Come back into the storage area with me. Take a look. And a listen."

"Customers are not allowed in the—"

"Bud," Ollie said, "go with him. Let's settle this."

"All right," Brown said. "Mr. Drayton? Let's get this foolishness over with."

We pushed through the double doors into the darkness.

The sound was unpleasant—perhaps evil.

Brown felt it, too, for all his hardheaded Yankee manner; his hand clutched my arm immediately, his breath caught for a moment and then resumed more harshly.

It was a low whispering sound from the direction of the loading door—an almost caressing sound. I swept around gently with one foot and finally struck one of the flashlights. I bent down, got it, and turned it on. Brown's face was tightly drawn, and he hadn't even seen them—he was only hearing them. But I had seen, and I could imagine them twisting and climbing over the corrugated steel surface of the door like living vines.

"What do you think now? Totally beyond belief?"

Brown licked his lips and looked at the littered confusion of boxes and bags. "They did this?"

"Some of it. Most of it. Come over here."

He came—reluctantly. I spotted the flashlight on the shriveled and curled section of tentacle, still lying by the push broom. Brown bent toward it.

"Don't touch that," I said. "It may still be alive."

He straightened up quickly. I picked up the broom by the bristles and prodded the tentacle. The third or fourth poke caused it to unclench sluggishly and reveal two whole suckers and a ragged segment of a third. Then the fragment coiled again with muscular speed and lay still. Brown made a gagging, disgusted sound.

"Seen enough?"

"Yes," he said. "Let's get out of here."

We followed the bobbing light back to the double doors and pushed through them. All the faces turned toward us, and the hum of conversation died. Norton's face was like old cheese. Mrs. Carmody's black eyes glinted. Ollie was drinking beer; his face was still running with trickles of perspiration, although it had gotten rather chilly in the market. The two girls with CAMP WOODLANDS on their shirts were huddled together like young horses before a thunderstorm. Eyes. So many eyes. I could paint them, I thought with a chill. No faces, only eyes in the gloom. I could paint them but no one would believe they were real.

Bud Brown folded his long-fingered hands primly in front of him. "People," he said. "It appears we have a problem of some magnitude here."

VI

Further Discussion. Mrs. Carmody. Fortifications. What Happened to the Flat-Earth Society.

The next four hours passed in a kind of dream. There was a long and semihysterical discussion following Brown's confirmation, or maybe the discussion wasn't as long as it seemed; maybe it was just the grim necessity of people chewing over the same information, trying to see it from every possible point of view, working it the way a dog works a bone, trying to get at the marrow. It was a slow coming to belief. You can see the same thing at any New England town meeting in March.

There was the Flat-Earth Society, headed by Norton. They were a vocal minority of about ten who believed none of it. Norton pointed out over and over again that there were only four witnesses to the bag-boy being carried off by what he called the Tentacles from Planet X (it was good for a laugh the first time, but it wore thin quickly; Norton, in his increasing agitation, seemed not to notice). He added that he personally did not trust one of the four. He further pointed out that fifty percent of the witnesses were now hopelessly inebriated. That was unquestionably true. Jim and Myron LaFleur, with the entire beer cooler and wine rack at their disposal, were abysmally shitfaced. Considering what had happened to Norm, and their part in it, I didn't blame them. They would sober off all too soon.

Ollie continued to drink steadily, ignoring Brown's protests. After a while Brown gave up, contenting himself with an occasional baleful threat about the Company. He didn't seem to realize that Federal Foods, Inc., with its stores in Bridgton, North Windham, and Portland, might not even exist anymore. For all we knew, the Eastern Seaboard might no longer exist. Ollie drank steadily, but didn't get drunk. He was sweating it out as rapidly as he could put it in.

At last, as the discussion with the Flat-Earthers was becoming acrimonious, Ollie spoke up. "If you don't believe it, Mr. Norton, that's fine. I'll tell you what to do. You go on out that front door and walk around to the back. There's a great big pile of returnable beer and soda bottles there. Norm and Buddy and I put them out this morning. You bring back a couple of those bottles so we know you really went back there. You do that and I'll personally take my shirt off and eat it."

Norton began to bluster.

Ollie cut him off in that same soft, even voice. "I tell you, you're not doing anything but damage talking the way you are. There's people here that want to go home and make sure their families are okay. My sister and her year-old daughter are at home in Naples right now. I'd like to check on them, sure. But if people start believing you and try to go home, what happened to Norm is going to happen to them."

He didn't convince Norton, but he convinced some of the leaners and fence sitters—it wasn't what he said so much as it was his eyes, his haunted eyes. I think Norton's sanity hinged on not being convinced, or that he thought it did. But he didn't take Ollie up on his offer to bring back a sampling of returnables from out back. None of them did. They weren't ready to go out, at least not yet. He and his little group of Flat-Earthers (reduced by one or two now) went as far away from the rest of us as they could get, over by the prepared-meats case. One of them kicked my sleeping son in the leg as he went past, waking him up.

I went over, and Billy clung to my neck. When I tried to put him down, he clung tighter and said, "Don't do that, Daddy. Please."

I found a shopping cart and put him in the baby seat. He looked very big in there. It would have been comical except for his pale face, the dark hair brushed across his forehead just above his eyebrows, his woeful eyes. He probably hadn't been up in the baby seat of the shopping cart for as long as two years. These little things slide by you, you don't realize at first, and when what has changed finally comes to you, it's always a nasty shock.

Meanwhile, with the Flat-Earthers having withdrawn, the argument had found another lightning rod—this time it was Mrs. Carmody, and understandably enough, she stood alone.

In the faded, dismal light she was witchlike in her blazing canary pants, her bright rayon blouse, her armloads of clacking junk jewelry—copper, tortoiseshell, adamantine—and her thyroidal purse. Her parchment face was grooved with strong vertical lines. Her frizzy gray hair was yanked flat with three horn combs and twisted in the back. Her mouth was a line of knotted rope.

"There is no defense against the will of God. This has been coming. I have seen the signs. There are those here that I have told, but there are none so blind as those who will not see."

"Well, what are you saying? What are you proposing?" Mike Hatlen broke in impatiently. He was a town selectman, although he didn't look the part now, in his yachtsman's cap and saggy-seated Bermudas. He was sipping at a beer; a great many men were doing it now. Bud Brown had given up protesting, but he was indeed taking names—keeping a rough tab on everyone he could.

"Proposing?" Mrs. Carmody echoed, wheeling toward Hatlen. "Proposing? Why, I am proposing that you prepare to meet your God, Michael Hatlen." She gazed around at all of us. "Prepare to meet your God!"

"Prepare to meet shit," Myron LaFleur said in a drunken snarl from the beer cooler. "Old woman, I believe your tongue must be hung in the middle so it can run on both ends."

There was a rumble of agreement. Billy looked around nervously, and I slipped an arm around his shoulders.

"I'll have my say!" she cried. Her upper lip curled back, revealing snaggle teeth that were yellow with nicotine. I thought of the dusty stuffed animals in her shop, drinking eternally at the mirror that served as their creek. "Doubters will doubt to the end! Yet a monstrosity did drag that poor boy away! Things in the mist! Every abomination out of a bad dream! Eyeless freaks! Pallid horrors! Do you doubt? Then go on out! Go on out and say howdy-do!"

"Mrs. Carmody, you'll have to stop," I said. "You're scaring my boy."

The man with the little girl echoed the sentiment. She, all plump legs and scabby knees, had hidden her face against her father's stomach and put her hands over her ears. Big Bill wasn't crying, but he was close.

"There's only one chance," Mrs. Carmody said.

"What's that, ma'am?" Mike Hatlen asked politely.

"A sacrifice," Mrs. Carmody said—she seemed to grin in the gloom. "A blood sacrifice."

Blood sacrifice—the words hung there, slowly turning. Even now, when I know better, I tell myself that then what she meant was someone's pet dog—there were a couple of them trotting around the market in spite of the regulations against them. Even now I tell myself that. She looked like some crazed remnant of

New England Puritanism in the gloom   but I
suspect that something deeper and darker than mere
Puritanism motivated her. Puritanism had its own
dark grandfather, old Adam with bloody hands.

She opened her mouth to say something more, and
a small, neat man in red pants and a natty sport shirt
struck her openhanded across the face. His hair was
parted with ruler evenness on the left. He wore
glasses. He also wore the unmistakable look of the
summer tourist.

"You shut up that bad talk," he said softly and
tonelessly.

Mrs. Carmody put her hand to her mouth and then
held it out to us, a wordless accusation. There was
blood on the palm. But her black eyes seemed to
dance with mad glee.

"You had it coming!" a woman cried out. "I would
have done it myself!"

"They'll get hold of you," Mrs. Carmody said,
showing us her bloody palm. The trickle of blood
was now running down one of the wrinkles from her
mouth to her chin like a droplet of rain down a gut-
ter. "Not today, maybe. Tonight. Tonight when the
dark comes. They'll come with the night and take
someone else. With the night they'll come. You'll
hear them coming, creeping and crawling. And when
they come, you'll beg for Mother Carmody to show
you what to do."

The man in the red pants raised his hand slowly.

"You come on and hit me," she whispered, and
grinned her bloody grin at him. His hand wavered.

"Hit me if you dare." His hand dropped. Mrs. Carmody walked away by herself. Then Billy did begin to cry, hiding his face against me as the little girl had done with her father.

"I want to go home," he said. "I want to see my mommy."

I comforted him as best I could. Which probably wasn't very well.

The talk finally turned into less frightening and destructive channels. The plate-glass windows, the market's obvious weak point, were mentioned. Mike Hatlen asked what other entrances there were, and Ollie and Brown quickly ticked them off—two loading doors in addition to the one Norm had opened. The main IN/OUT doors. The window in the manager's office (thick, reinforced glass, securely locked).

Talking about these things had a paradoxical effect. It made the danger seem more real but at the same time made us feel better. Even Billy felt it. He asked if he could go get a candy bar. I told him it would be all right so long as he didn't go near the big windows.

When he was out of earshot, a man near Mike Hatlen said, "Okay, what are we going to do about those windows? The old lady may be as crazy as a bedbug, but she could be right about something moving in after dark."

"Maybe the fog will blow over by then," a woman said.

"Maybe," the man said. "And maybe not."

"Any ideas?" I asked Bud and Ollie.

"Hold on a sec," the man near Hatlen said. "I'm Dan Miller. From Lynn, Mass. You don't know me, no reason why you should, but I got a place on Highland Lake. Bought it just this year. Got held up for it, is more like it, but I had to have it." There were a few chuckles. "Anyway, I saw a whole pile of fertilizer and lawn-food bags down there. Twenty-five-pound sacks, most of them. We could put them up like sandbags. Leave loopholes to look out through. . . ."

Now more people were nodding and talking excitedly. I almost said something, then held it back. Miller was right. Putting those bags up could do no harm, and might do some good. But my mind went back to that tentacle squeezing the dog-food bag. I thought that one of the bigger tentacles could probably do the same for a twenty-five-pound bag of Green Acres lawn food or Vigoro. But a sermon on that wouldn't get us out or improve anyone's mood.

People began to break up, talking about getting it done, and Miller yelled: "Hold it! Hold it! Let's thrash this out while we're all together!"

They came back, a loose congregation of fifty or sixty people in the corner formed by the beer cooler, the storage doors, and the left end of the meat case, where Mr. McVey always seems to put the things no one wants, like sweetbreads and Scotch eggs and sheep's brains and head cheese. Billy wove his way through them with a five-year-old's unconscious agility in a world of giants and held up a Hershey bar. "Want this, Daddy?"

"Thanks." I took it. It tasted sweet and good.

"This is probably a stupid question," Miller resumed, "but we ought to fill in the blanks. Anyone got any firearms?"

There was a pause. People looked around at each other and shrugged. An old man with grizzled white hair who introduced himself as Ambrose Cornell said he had a shotgun in the trunk of his car. "I'll try for it, if you want."

Ollie said, "Right now I don't think that would be a good idea, Mr. Cornell."

Cornell grunted. "Right now, neither do I, son. But I thought I ought to make the offer."

"Well, I didn't really think so," Dan Miller said. "But I thought—"

"Wait, hold it a minute," a woman said. It was the lady in the cranberry-colored sweatshirt and the dark green slacks. She had sandy-blond hair and a good figure. A very pretty young woman. She opened her purse and from it she produced a medium-sized pistol. The crowd made an *ahhhh*-ing sound, as if they had just seen a magician do a particularly fine trick. The woman, who had been blushing, blushed that much the harder. She rooted in her purse again and brought out a box of Smith & Wesson ammunition.

"I'm Amanda Dumfries," she said to Miller. "This gun . . . my husband's idea. He thought I should have it for protection. I've carried it unloaded for two years."

"Is your husband here, ma'am?"

"No, he's in New York. On business. He's gone on business a lot. That's why he wanted me to carry the gun."

"Well," Miller said, "if you can use it, you ought to keep it. What is it, a thirty-eight?"

"Yes. And I've never fired it in my life except on a target range once."

Miller took the gun, fumbled around, and got the cylinder to open after a few moments. He checked to make sure it was not loaded. "Okay," he said. "We got a gun. Who shoots good? I sure don't."

People glanced at each other. No one said anything at first. Then, reluctantly, Ollie said: "I target-shoot quite a lot. I have a Colt .45 and a Llama .25."

"You?" Brown said. "Huh. You'll be too drunk to see by dark."

Ollie said very clearly, "Why don't you just shut up and write down your names?"

Brown goggled at him. Opened his mouth. Then decided, wisely, I think, to shut it again.

"It's yours," Miller said, blinking a little at the exchange. He handed it over and Ollie checked it again, more professionally. He put the gun into his right-front pants pocket and slipped the cartridge box into his breast pocket, where it made a bulge like a pack of cigarettes. Then he leaned back against the cooler, round face still trickling sweat, and cracked a fresh

beer. The sensation that I was seeing a totally unsus-
pected Ollie Weeks persisted.

"Thank you, Mrs. Dumfries," Miller said.

"Don't mention it," she said, and I thought fleet-
ingly that if I were her husband and proprietor of
those green eyes and that full figure, I might not
travel so much. Giving your wife a gun could be
seen as a ludicrously symbolic act.

"This may be silly, too," Miller said, turning back
to Brown with his clipboard and Ollie with his beer,
"but there aren't anything like flamethrowers in the
place, are there?"

"Ohhh, *shit*," Buddy Eagleton said, and then went
as red as Amanda Dumfries had done.

"What is it?" Mike Hatlen asked.

"Well . . . until last week we had a whole case of
those little blowtorches. The kind you use around
your house to solder leaky pipes or mend your exhaust systems or whatever. You remember those,
Mr. Brown?"

Brown nodded, looking sour.

"Sold out?" Miller asked.

"No, they didn't go at all. We only sold three or
four and sent the rest of the case back. What a pisser.
I mean . . . what a shame." Blushing so deeply he
was almost purple, Buddy Eagleton retired into the
background again.

We had matches, of course, and salt (someone said
vaguely that he had heard salt was the thing to put
on bloodsuckers and things like that); and all kinds

of O'Cedar mops and long-handled brooms. Most of
the people continued to look heartened, and Jim and
Myron were too blotzo to sound a dissenting note,
but I met Ollie's eyes and saw a calm hopelessness
in them that was worse than fear. He and I had seen
the tentacles. The idea of throwing salt on them or
trying to fend them off with the handles of O'Cedar
mops was funny, in a ghastly way.

"Mike," Miller said, "why don't you crew this little
adventure? I want to talk to Ollie and Dave here for
a minute."

"Glad to." Hatlen clapped Dan Miller on the
shoulder. "Somebody had to take charge, and you
did it good. Welcome to town."

"Does this mean I get a kickback on my taxes?"
Miller asked. He was a banty little guy with red hair
that was receding. He looked like the sort of guy you
can't help liking on short notice and—just maybe—
the kind of guy you can't help not liking after he's
been around for a while. The kind of guy who knows
how to do everything better than you do.

"No way," Hatlen said, laughing.

Hatlen walked off. Miller glanced down at my son.

"Don't worry about Billy," I said.

"Man, I've never been so worried in my whole
life," Miller said.

"No," Ollie agreed, and dropped an empty into
the beer cooler. He got a fresh one and opened it.
There was a soft hiss of escaping gas.

"I got a look at the way you two glanced at each
other," Miller said.

I finished my Hershey bar and got a beer to wash it down with.

"Tell you what I think," Miller said. "We ought to get half a dozen people to wrap some of those mop handles with cloth and then tie them down with twine. Then I think we ought to get a couple of those cans of charcoal lighter fluid all ready. If we cut the tops right off the cans, we could have some torches pretty quick,"

I nodded. That was good. Almost surely not good enough—not if you had seen Norm dragged out—but it was better than salt.

"That would give them something to think about, at least," Ollie said.

Miller's lips pressed together. "That bad, huh?" he said.

"That bad," Ollie agreed, and worked his beer.

By four-thirty that afternoon the sacks of fertilizer and lawn food were in place and the big windows were blocked off except for narrow loopholes. A watchman had been placed at each of these, and beside each watchman was a tin of charcoal lighter fluid with the top cut off and a supply of mop-handle torches. There were five loopholes, and Dan Miller had arranged a rotation of sentries for each one. When four-thirty came around, I was sitting on a pile of bags at one of the loopholes, Billy at my side. We were looking out into the mist.

Just beyond the window was a red bench where people sometimes waited for their rides with their groceries beside them. Beyond that was the parking lot. The mist swirled slowly, thick and heavy. There *was* moisture in it, but how dull it seemed, and gloomy. Just looking at it made me feel gutless and lost.

"Daddy, do you know what's happening?" Billy asked.

"No, hon," I said.

He fell silent for a bit, looking at his hands, which lay limply in the lap of his Tuffskin jeans. "Why doesn't somebody come and rescue us?" he asked finally. "The State Police or the FBI or someone?"

"I don't know."

"Do you think Mom's okay?"

"Billy, I just don't know," I said, and put an arm around him.

"I want her awful bad," Billy said, struggling with tears. "I'm sorry about the times I was bad to her."

"Billy," I said, and had to stop. I could taste salt in my throat, and my voice wanted to tremble.

"Will it be over?" Billy asked. "Daddy? Will it?"

"I don't know," I said, and he put his face in the hollow of my shoulder and I held the back of his head, felt the delicate curve of his skull just under the thick growth of his hair. I found myself remembering the evening of my wedding day. Watching Steff take off the simple brown dress she had changed into after the ceremony. She had had a big purple bruise on one hip from running into the side of a door the day before. I remembered looking at the bruise and thinking, *When she got that, she was still Stephanie Stepanek*, and feeling something like wonder. Then we had made love, and outside it was spitting snow from a dull gray December sky.

Billy was crying.

"Shh, Billy, shh," I said, rocking his head against me, but he went on crying. It was the sort of crying that only mothers know how to fix right.

Premature night came inside the Federal Foods. Miller and Hatlen and Bud Brown handed out flashlights, the whole stock, about twenty. Norton clamored loudly for them on behalf of his group, and received two. The lights bobbed here and there in the aisles like uneasy phantoms.

I held Billy against me and looked out through the loophole. The milky, translucent quality of the light out there hadn't changed much; it was putting up the bags that had made the market so dark. Several times I thought I saw something, but it was only jumpiness. One of the others raised a hesitant false alarm.

Billy saw Mrs. Turman again, and went to her eagerly, even though she hadn't been over to sit for him all summer. She had one of the flashlights and handed it over to him amiably enough. Soon he was trying to write his name in light on the blank glass faces of the frozen-food cases. She seemed as happy to see him as he was to see her, and in a little while they came over. Hattie Turman was a tall, thin woman with lovely red hair just beginning to streak gray. A pair of glasses hung from an ornamental chain—the sort, I believe, it is illegal for anyone except middle-aged women to wear—on her breast.

"Is Stephanie here, David?" she asked.

"No. At home."

She nodded. "Alan, too. How long are you on watch here?"

"Until six."

"Have you seen anything?"

"No. Just the mist."

"I'll keep Billy until six, if you like."

"Would you like that, Billy?"

"Yes, please," he said, swinging the flashlight above his head in slow arcs and watching it play across the ceiling.

"God will keep your Steffy, and Alan, too," Mrs. Turman said, and led Billy away by the hand. She spoke with serene sureness, but there was no conviction in her eyes.

Around five-thirty the sounds of excited argument rose near the back of the store. Someone jeered at something someone else had said, and someone—it was Buddy Eagleton, I think—shouted, "You're crazy if you go out there!"

Several of the flashlight beams pooled together at the center of the controversy, and they moved toward the front of the store. Mrs. Carmody's shrieking, derisive laugh split the gloom, as abrasive as fingers drawn down a slate blackboard.

Above the babble of voices came the boom of Norton's courtroom tenor: "Let us pass, please! Let us pass!"

The man at the loophole next to mine left his place to see what the shouting was about. I decided to stay where I was. Whatever the concatenation was, it was coming my way.

"Please," Mike Hatlen was saying. "Please, let's talk this thing through."

"There is nothing to talk about," Norton proclaimed. Now his face swam out of the gloom. It was determined and haggard and wholly wretched. He was holding one of the two flashlights allocated to the Flat-Earthers. The corkscrewed tufts of hair still stuck up behind his ears like a cuckold's horns. He was at the head of an extremely small procession—five of the original nine or ten. "We are going out," he said.

"Don't stick to this craziness," Miller said. "Mike's right. We can talk it over, can't we? Mr. McVey is going to barbecue some chicken over the gas grill, we can all sit down and eat and just—"

He got in Norton's way and Norton gave him a push. Miller didn't like it. His face flushed and then set in a hard expression. "Do what you want, then," he said. "But you're as good as murdering these other people."

With all the evenness of great resolve or unbreakable obsession, Norton said: "We'll send help back for you."

One of his followers murmured agreement, but another quietly slipped away. Now there was Norton and four others. Maybe that wasn't so bad. Christ Himself could only find twelve.

"Listen," Mike Hatlen said. "Mr. Norton—Brent—at least stay for the chicken. Get some hot food inside you."

"And give you a chance to go on talking? I've been in too many courtrooms to fall for that. You've psyched out half a dozen of my people already."

"Your people?" Hatlen almost groaned it. "*Your* people? Good Christ, what kind of talk is that? They're *people*, that's all. This is no game, and it's surely not a courtroom. There are, for want of a better word, there are *things* out there, and what's the sense of getting yourself killed?"

"Things, you say," Norton said, sounding superficially amused. "Where? Your people have been on watch for a couple of hours now. Who's seen one?"

"Well, out back. In the—"

"No, no, no," Norton said, shaking his head. "That ground has been covered and covered. We're going out—"

"No," someone whispered, and it echoed and spread, sounding like the rustle of dead leaves at dusk of an October evening. *No, no, no . . .*

"Will you restrain us?" a shrill voice asked. This was one of Norton's "people," to use his word—an elderly lady wearing bifocals. "Will you restrain us?"

The soft babble of negatives died away.

"No," Mike said. "No, I don't think anyone will restrain you."

I whispered in Billy's ear. He looked at me, startled and questioning. "Go on, now," I said. "Be quick."

He went.

Norton ran his hands through his hair, a gesture as calculated as any ever made by a Broadway actor. I had liked him better pulling the cord of his chainsaw fruitlessly, cussing and thinking himself unobserved. I could not tell then and do not know any better now if he believed in what he was doing or not. I think, down deep, that he knew what was going to happen. I think that the logic he had paid lip service to all his life turned on him at the end like a tiger that has gone bad and mean.

He looked around restlessly, seeming to wish that there was more to say. Then he led his four followers through one of the checkout lanes. In addition to the elderly woman, there was a chubby boy of about twenty, a young girl, and a man in blue jeans wearing a golf cap tipped back on his head.

Norton's eyes caught mine, widened a little, and then started to swing away.

"Brent, wait a minute," I said.

"I don't want to discuss it any further. Certainly not with you."

"I know you don't. I just want to ask a favor." I looked around and saw Billy coming back toward the checkouts at a run.

"What's that?" Norton asked suspiciously as Billy came up and handed me a package done up in cellophane.

"Clothesline," I said. I was vaguely aware that everyone in the market was watching us now, loosely strung out on the other side of the cash registers and checkout lanes. "It's the big package. Three hundred feet."

"So?"

"I wondered if you'd tie one end around your waist before you go out. I'll let it out. When you feel it come up tight, just tie it around something. It doesn't matter what. A car door handle would do."

"What in God's name for?"

"It will tell me you got at least three hundred feet," I said.

Something in his eyes flickered . . . but only momentarily. "No," he said.

I shrugged. "Okay. Good luck, anyhow."

Abruptly the man in the golf cap said, "I'll do it, mister. No reason not to."

Norton swung on him, as if to say something sharp, and the man in the golf cap studied him calmly. There was nothing flickering in *his* eyes. He had made his decision and there was simply no doubt in him. Norton saw it too and said nothing.

"Thanks," I said.

I slit the wrapping with my pocketknife and the clothesline accordioned out in stiff loops. I found one loose end and tied it around Golf Cap's waist in a loose granny. He immediately untied it and cinched it tighter with a good quick sheet-bend knot. There was not a sound in the market. Norton shifted uneasily from foot to foot.

"You want to take my knife?" I asked the man in the golf cap.

"I got one." He looked at me with that same calm contempt. "You just see to paying out your line. If it binds up, I'll chuck her."

"Are we all ready?" Norton asked, too loud. The chubby boy jumped as if he had been goosed. Getting no response, Norton turned to go.

"Brent," I said, and held out my hand. "Good luck, man."

He studied my hand as if it were some dubious foreign object. "We'll send back help," he said finally, and pushed through the OUT door. That thin, acrid smell came in again. The others followed him out.

Mike Hatlen came down and stood beside me. Norton's party of five stood in the milky, slow-moving fog. Norton said something and I should have heard it, but the mist seemed to have an odd damping effect. I heard nothing but the sound of his voice and two or three isolated syllables, like the voice on the radio heard from some distance. They moved off.

Hatlen held the door a little way open. I paid out the clothesline, keeping as much slack in it as I could, mindful of the man's promise to chuck the rope if it bound him up. There was still not a sound. Billy stood beside me, motionless but seeming to thrum with his own inner current.

Again there was that weird feeling that the five of them did not so much disappear into the fog as become invisible. For a moment their clothes seemed to stand alone, and then they were gone. You were not really impressed with the unnatural density of the mist until you saw people swallowed up in a space of seconds.

I paid the line out. A quarter of it went, then a half. It stopped going out for a moment. It went from a live thing to a dead one in my hands. I held my breath. Then it started to go out again. I paid it through my fingers, and suddenly remembered my father taking me to see the Gregory Peck film of *Moby-Dick* at the Brookside. I think I smiled a little.

Three-quarters of the line was gone now. I could see the end of it lying beside one of Billy's feet. Then the rope stopped moving through my hands again. It lay motionless for perhaps five seconds, and then another five feet jerked out. Then it suddenly whipsawed violently to the left, twanging off the edge of the OUT door.

Twenty feet of rope suddenly paid out, making a thin heat across my left palm. And from out of the mist there came a high, wavering scream. It was impossible to tell the sex of the screamer.

The rope whipsawed in my hands again. And again. It skated across the space in the doorway to the right, then back to the left. A few more feet paid out, and then there was a ululating howl from out there that brought an answering moan from my son. Hatlen stood aghast. His eyes were huge. One corner of his mouth turned down, trembling.

The howl was abruptly cut off. There was no sound at all for what seemed to be forever. Then the old lady cried out—this time there could be no doubt about who it was. *"Git it offa me!"* she screamed. *"Oh my Lord my Lord get it—"*

Then her voice was cut off, too.

Almost all of the rope abruptly ran out through my loosely closed fist, giving me a hotter burn this time. Then it went completely slack, and a sound came out of the mist—a thick, loud grunt—that made all the spit in my mouth dry up.

It was like no sound I've ever heard, but the closest approximation might be a movie set in the African veld or a South American swamp. It was the sound of a big animal. It came again, low and tearing and savage. Once more . . . and then it subsided to a series of low mutterings. Then it was completely gone.

"Close the door," Amanda Dumfries said in a trembling voice. "Please."

"In a minute," I said, and began to yank the line back in.

It came out of the mist and piled up around my feet in untidy loops and snarls. About three feet from the end, the new white clothesline went barn-red.

"Death!" Mrs. Carmody screamed. "Death to go out there! Now do you see?"

The end of the clothesline was a chewed and frayed tangle of fiber and little puffs of cotton. The little puffs were dewed with minute drops of blood.

No one contradicted Mrs. Carmody.

Mike Hatlen let the door swing shut.

VII

The First Night.

Mr. McVey had worked in Bridgton cutting meat ever since I was twelve or thirteen, and I had no idea what his first name was or his age might be. He had set up a gas grill under one of the small exhaust fans—the fans were still now, but presumably they still gave some ventilation—and by 6:30 P.M. the smell of cooking chicken filled the market. Bud Brown didn't object. It might have been shock, but more likely he had recognized the fact that his fresh meat and poultry wasn't getting any fresher. The chicken smelled good, but not many people wanted to eat. Mr. McVey, small and spare and neat in his whites, cooked the chicken nevertheless and laid the pieces two by two on paper plates and lined them up cafeteria-style on top of the meat counter.

Mrs. Turman brought Billy and me each a plate, garnished with helpings of deli potato salad. I ate as best I could, but Billy would not even pick at his.

"You got to eat, big guy," I said.

"I'm not hungry," he said, putting the plate aside.

"You can't get big and strong if you don't—"

Mrs. Turman, sitting slightly behind Billy, shook her head at me.

"Okay," I said. "Go get a peach and eat it, at least. 'Kay?"

"What if Mr. Brown says something?"

"If he says something, you come back and tell me."

"Okay, Dad."

He walked away slowly. He seemed to have shrunk somehow. It hurt my heart to see him walk that way. Mr. McVey went on cooking chicken, apparently not minding that only a few people were eating it, happy in the act of cooking. As I think I have said, there are all ways of handling a thing like this. You wouldn't think it would be so, but it is. The mind is a monkey.

Mrs. Turman and I sat halfway up the patent-medicines aisle. People were sitting in little groups all over the store. No one except Mrs. Carmody was sitting alone; even Myron and his buddy Jim were together—they were both passed out by the beer cooler.

Six new men were watching the loopholes. One of them was Ollie, gnawing a leg of chicken and drinking a beer. The mop-handle torches leaned beside each of the watchposts, a can of charcoal lighter fluid next to each . . . but I don't think anyone really believed in the torches the way they had before. Not after that low and terribly vital grunting sound, not after the chewed and blood-soaked clothesline. If whatever was out there decided it wanted us, it was going to have us. It, or they.

"How bad will it be tonight?" Mrs. Turman asked. Her voice was calm, but her eyes were sick and scared.

"Hattie, I just don't know."

"You let me keep Billy as much as you can. I'm . . . Davey, I think I'm in mortal terror." She uttered a dry laugh. "Yes, I believe that's what it is. But if I have Billy, I'll be all right. I'll be all right for him."

Her eyes were glistening. I leaned over and patted her shoulder.

"I'm so worried about Alan," she said. "He's dead, Davey. In my heart, I'm sure he's dead."

"No, Hattie. You don't know any such thing."

"But I feel it's true. Don't you feel anything about Stephanie? Don't you at least have a . . . a feeling?"

"No," I said, lying through my teeth.

A strangled sound came from her throat and she clapped a hand to her mouth. Her glasses reflected back the dim, murky light.

"Billy's coming back," I murmured.

He was eating a peach. Hattie Turman patted the floor beside her and said that when he was done she would show him how to make a little man out of the peach pit and some thread. Billy smiled at her wanly, and Mrs. Turman smiled back.

At 8:00 P.M. six new men went on at the loopholes and Ollie came over to where I was sitting. "Where's Billy?"

"With Mrs. Turman, up back," I said. "They're doing crafts. They've run through peach-pit men and shopping-bag masks and apple dolls and now Mr. McVey is showing him how to make pipe-cleaner men."

Ollie took a long drink of beer and said, "Things are moving around out there."

I looked at him sharply. He looked back levelly.

"I'm not drunk," he said. "I've been trying but haven't been able to make it. I wish I could, David."

"What do you mean, things are moving around out there?"

"I can't say for sure. I asked Walter, and he said he had the same feeling, that parts of the mist would go darker for a minute—sometimes just a little smudge, sometimes a big dark place, like a bruise. Then it would fade back to gray. And the stuff is swirling around. Even Arnie Simms said he felt like something was going on out there, and Arnie's almost as blind as a bat."

"What about the others?"

"They're all out-of-staters, strangers to me," Ollie said. "I didn't ask any of them."

"How sure are you that you weren't just seeing things?"

"Sure," he said. He nodded toward Mrs. Carmody, who was sitting by herself at the end of the aisle. None of it had hurt her appetite any; there was a graveyard of chicken bones on her plate. She was drinking either blood or V-8 juice. "I think she was right about one thing," Ollie said. "We'll find out. When it gets dark, we'll find out."

But we didn't have to wait until dark. When it came, Billy saw very little of it, because Mrs. Turman kept him up back. Ollie was still sitting with me when one of the men up front gave out a shriek and staggered back from his post, pinwheeling his arms. It was approaching eight-thirty; outside the pearl-white mist had darkened to the dull slaty color of a November twilight.

Something had landed on the glass outside one of the loopholes.

"Oh my Jesus!" the man who had been watching there screamed. *"Let me out! Let me out of this!"*

He tore around in a rambling circle, his eyes starting from his face, a thin lick of saliva at one corner of his mouth glimmering in the deepening shadows. Then he took off straight up the far aisle past the frozen-food cases.

There were answering cries. Some people ran toward the front to see what had happened. Many others retreated toward the back, not caring and not wanting to see whatever was crawling on the glass out there.

I started down toward the loophole, Ollie by my side. His hand was in the pocket that held Mrs. Dumfries' gun. Now one of the other watchers let out a cry—not so much of fear as disgust.

Ollie and I slipped through one of the checkout

lanes. Now I could see what had frightened the guy from his post. I couldn't tell what it was, but I could see it. It looked like one of the minor creatures in a Bosch painting—one of his hellacious murals. There was something almost horribly comic about it, too, because it also looked a little like one of those strange creations of vinyl and plastic you can buy for $1.89 to spring on your friends . . . in fact, exactly the sort of thing Norton had accused me of planting in the storage area.

It was maybe two feet long, segmented, the pinkish color of burned flesh that has healed over. Bulbous eyes peered in two different directions at once from the ends of short, limber stalks. It clung to the window on fat sucker-pads. From the opposite end there protruded something that was either a sexual organ or a stinger. And from its back there sprouted over-sized, membranous wings, like the wings of a house-fly. They were moving very slowly as Ollie and I approached the glass.

At the loophole to the left of us, where the man had made the disgusted cawing sound, three of the things were crawling on the glass. They moved sluggishly across it, leaving sticky snail trails behind them. Their eyes—if that is what they were—joggled on the end of the finger-thick stalks. The biggest was maybe four feet long. At times they crawled right over each other.

"Look at those goddamn things," Tom Smalley said in a sickened voice. He was standing at the loophole on our right. I didn't reply. The bugs were all over the loopholes now, which meant they were probably crawling all over the building . . . like maggots on a piece of meat. It wasn't a pleasant image, and I could feel what chicken I had managed to eat now wanting to come up.

Someone was sobbing. Mrs. Carmody was screaming about abominations from within the earth. Someone told her gruffly that she'd shut up if she knew what was good for her. Same old shit.

Ollie took Mrs. Dumfries' gun from his pocket and I grabbed his arm. "Don't be crazy."

He shook free. "I know what I'm doing," he said.

He tapped the barrel of the gun on the window, his face set in a nearly masklike expression of distaste. The speed of the creatures' wings increased until they were only a blur—if you hadn't known, you might have believed they weren't winged creatures at all. Then they simply flew away.

Some of the others saw what Ollie had done and got the idea. They used the mop handles to tap on the windows. The things flew away, but came right back. Apparently they had no more brains than your average housefly, either. The near-panic dissolved in a babble of conversation. I heard someone asking someone else what he thought those things would do if they landed on you. That was a question I had no interest in seeing answered.

The tapping on the windows began to die away. Ollie turned toward me and started to say something, but before he could do more than open his mouth, something came out of the fog and snatched one of the crawling things off the glass. I think I screamed. I'm not sure.

It was a flying thing. Beyond that I could not have said for sure. The fog appeared to darken in exactly the way Ollie had described, only the dark smutch didn't fade away; it solidified into something with flapping, leathery wings, an albino white body, and reddish eyes. It thudded into the glass hard enough to make it shiver. Its beak opened. It scooped the pink thing in and was gone. The whole incident took no more than five seconds. I had a bare final impression of the pink thing wiggling and flapping as it went down the hatch, the way a small fish will wiggle and flap in the beak of a seagull.

Now there was another thud, and yet another. People began screaming again, and there was a stampede toward the back of the store. Then there was a more piercing scream, one of pain, and Ollie said, "Oh my God, that old lady fell down and they just ran over her."

He ran back through the checkout aisle. I turned to follow, and then I saw something that stopped me dead where I was standing.

High up and to my right, one of the lawn-food bags was sliding slowly backward. Tom Smalley was right under it, staring out into the mist through his loophole.

Another of the pink bugs landed on the thick plate glass of the loophole where Ollie and I had been standing. One of the flying things swooped down and grabbed it. The old woman who had been trampled went on screaming in a shrill, cracked voice.

That bag. That sliding bag.

"Smalley!" I shouted. "Look out! Heads up!"

In the general confusion, he never heard me. The bag teetered, then fell. It struck him squarely on the head. He went down hard, catching his jaw on the shelf that ran below the show window.

One of the albino flying things was squirming its way through the jagged hole in the glass. I could hear the soft scraping sound that it made, now that some of the screaming had stopped. Its red eyes glittered in its triangular head, which was slightly cocked to one side. A heavy, hooked beak opened and closed rapaciously. It looked a bit like the paintings of pterodactyls you may have seen in the dinosaur books, more like something out of a lunatic's nightmare.

I grabbed one of the torches and slam-dunked it into a can of charcoal lighter fluid, tipping it over and spilling a pool of the stuff across the floor.

The flying creature paused on top of the lawn-food bags, glaring around, shifting slowly and malignantly from one taloned foot to the other. It was a stupid creature, I am quite sure of that. Twice it tried to spread its wings, which struck the walls and then folded themselves over its hunched back like the wings of a griffin. The third time it tried, it lost its balance and fell clumsily from its perch, still trying to spread its wings. It landed on Tom Smalley's back.

One flex of its claws and Tom's shirt ripped wide open. Blood began to flow.

I was there, less than three feet away. My torch was dripping lighter fluid. I was emotionally pumped up to kill it if I could . . . and then realized I had no matches to light it with. I had used the last one lighting a cigar for Mr. McVey an hour ago.

The place was in pandemonium now. People had seen the thing roosting on Smalley's back, something no one in the world had seen before. It darted its head forward at a questing angle, and tore a chunk of meat from the back of Smalley's neck.

I was getting ready to use the torch as a bludgeon when the cloth-wrapped head of it suddenly blazed alight. Dan Miller was there, holding a Zippo lighter with a Marine emblem on it. His face was as harsh as a rock with horror and fury.

"Kill it," he said hoarsely. "Kill it if you can." Standing beside him was Ollie. He had Mrs. Dumfries' .38 in his hand, but he had no clear shot.

The thing spread its wings and flapped them once—apparently not to fly away but to secure a better hold on its prey—and then its leathery-white, membranous wings enfolded poor Smalley's entire upper body. Then the sounds came—mortal tearing sounds that I cannot bear to describe in any detail.

All of this happened in bare seconds. Then I thrust my torch at the thing. There was the sensation of striking something with no more real substance than a box kite. The next moment the entire creature was blazing. It made a screeching sound and its wings spread; its head jerked and its reddish eyes rolled with what I most sincerely hope was great agony. It took off with a sound like linen bedsheets flapping on a clothesline in a stiff spring breeze. It uttered that rusty shrieking sound again.

Heads turned up to follow its flaming, dying course. I think that nothing in the entire business stands in my memory so strongly as that bird-thing blazing a zigzagging course above the aisles of the Federal Supermarket, dropping charred and smoking bits of itself here and there. It finally crashed into the spaghetti sauces, splattering Ragú and Prince and Prima Salsa everywhere like gouts of blood. It was little more than ash and bone. The smell of its burning was high and sickening. And underlying it like a counterpoint was the thin and acrid stench of the mist, eddying in through the broken place in the glass.

For a moment there was utter silence. We were united in the black wonder of that brightly flaming deathflight. Then someone howled. Others screamed. And from somewhere in the back I could hear my son crying.

A hand grabbed me. It was Bud Brown. His eyes were bulging from their sockets. His lips were drawn back from his false teeth in a snarl. "One of those other things," he said, and pointed.

One of the bugs had come in through the hole and it now perched on a lawn-food bag, housefly wings buzzing—you could hear them; it sounded like a cheap department-store electric fan—eyes bulging from their stalks. Its pink and noxiously plump body was aspirating rapidly.

I moved toward it. My torch was guttering but not yet out. But Mrs. Reppler, the third-grade teacher, beat me to it. She was maybe fifty-five, maybe sixty, rope-thin. Her body had a tough, dried-out look that always makes me think of beef jerky.

She had a can of Raid in each hand like some crazy gunslinger in an existential comedy. She uttered a snarl of anger that would have done credit to a caveman splitting the skull of an enemy. Holding the pressure cans out at the full length of each arm, she pressed the buttons. A thick spray of insect-killer coated the thing. It went into throes of agony, twisting and turning crazily and at last falling from the bags, bouncing off the body of Tom Smalley—who was dead beyond any doubt or question—and finally landing on the floor. Its wings buzzed madly, but they weren't taking it anywhere; they were too heavily coated with Raid. A few moments later the wings slowed, then stopped. It was dead.

You could hear people crying now. And moaning. The old lady who had been trampled was moaning. And you could hear laughter. The laughter of the damned. Mrs. Reppler stood over her kill, her thin chest rising and falling rapidly.

Hatlen and Miller had found one of those dollies that the stockboys use to trundle cases of things around the store, and together they heaved it atop the lawn-food bags, blocking off the wedge-shaped hole in the glass. As a temporary measure, it was a good one.

Amanda Dumfries came forward like a sleep-walker. In one hand she held a plastic floor bucket. In the other she held a whisk broom, still done up in its see-through wrapping. She bent, her eyes still wide and blank, and swept the dead pink thing—bug, slug, whatever it was—into the bucket. You could hear the crackle of the wrapping on the whisk broom as it brushed the floor. She walked over to the OUT door. There were none of the bugs on it. She opened it a little way and threw the bucket out. It landed on its side and rolled back and forth in ever-decreasing arcs. One of the pink things buzzed out of the night, landed on the floor pail, and began to crawl over it.

Amanda burst into tears. I walked over and put an arm around her shoulders.

At one-thirty the following morning I was sitting with my back against the white enamel side of the meat counter in a semidoze. Billy's head was in my lap. He was solidly asleep. Not far away Amanda Dumfries was sleeping with her head pillowed on someone's jacket.

Not long after the flaming death of the bird-thing, Ollie and I had gone back out to the storage area and had gathered up half a dozen of the pads such as the one I'd covered Billy with earlier. Several people were sleeping on these. We had also brought back several heavy crates of oranges and pears, and four of us working together had been able to swing them to the tops of the lawn-food bags in front of the hole in the glass. The bird-creatures would have a tough time shifting one of those crates; they weighed about ninety pounds each.

But the birds and the buglike things the birds ate weren't the only things out there. There was the tentacled thing that had taken Norm. There was the frayed clothesline to think about. There was the unseen thing that had uttered that low, guttural roar to think about. We had heard sounds like it since—sometimes quite distant—but how far was "distant" through the damping effect of the mist? And sometimes they were close enough to shake the building and make it seem as if the ventricles of your heart had suddenly been loaded up with ice water.

Billy started in my lap and moaned. I brushed his hair and he moaned more loudly. Then he seemed to find sleep's less dangerous waters again. My own doze was broken and I was staring wide awake again. Since dark, I had only managed to sleep about ninety minutes, and that had been dream-haunted. In one of the dream fragments it had been the night before again. Billy and Steffy were standing in front of the picture window, looking out at the black and slate gray waters, out at the silver spinning waterspout that heralded the storm. I tried to get to them, knowing that a strong enough wind could break the window and throw deadly glass darts all the way across the living room. But no matter how I ran, I seemed to get no closer to them. And then a bird rose out of the waterspout, a gigantic scarlet *oiseau de mort* whose prehistoric wingspan darkened the entire lake from west to east. Its beak opened, revealing a maw the size of the Holland Tunnel. And as the bird came to gobble up my wife and son, a low, sinister voice began to whisper over and over again: *The Arrowhead Project . . . the Arrowhead Project . . . the Arrowhead Project . . .*

Not that Billy and I were the only ones sleeping poorly. Others screamed in their sleep, and some went on screaming after they woke up. The beer was disappearing from the cooler at a great rate. Buddy Eagleton had restocked it once from out back with no comment. Mike Hatlen told me the Sominex was gone. Not depleted but totally wiped out. He guessed that some people might have taken six or eight bottles.

"There's some Nytol left," he said. "You want a bottle, David?" I shook my head and thanked him.

And in the last aisle down by Register 5, we had our winos. There were about seven of them, all out-of-staters except for Lou Tattinger, who ran the Pine Tree Car Wash. Lou didn't need any excuse to sniff the cork, as the saying was. The wino brigade was pretty well anesthetized.

Oh yes—there were also six or seven people who had gone crazy.

Crazy isn't the best word; perhaps I just can't think of the proper one. But there were these people who had lapsed into a complete stupor without benefit of beer, wine, or pills. They stared at you with blank and shiny doorknob eyes. The hard cement of reality had come apart in some unimaginable earthquake, and these poor devils had fallen through. In time, some of them might come back. If there was time.

The rest of us had made our own mental compromises, and in some cases I suppose they were fairly odd. Mrs. Reppler, for instance, was convinced the whole thing was a dream—or so she said. And she spoke with some conviction.

I looked over at Amanda. I was developing an uncomfortably strong feeling for her—uncomfortable but not exactly unpleasant. Her eyes were an incredible brilliant green . . . for a while I had kept an eye on her to see if she was going to take out a pair of contact lenses, but apparently the color was true. I wanted to make love to her. My wife was at home, maybe alive, more probably dead, alone either way, and I loved her; I wanted to get Billy and me back to her more than anything, but I also wanted to screw this lady named Amanda Dumfries. I tried to tell myself it was just the situation we were in, and maybe it was, but that didn't change the wanting.

I dozed in and out, then jerked awake more fully around three. Amanda had shifted into a sort of fetal position, her knees pulled up toward her chest, hands clasped between her thighs. She seemed to be sleeping deeply. Her sweatshirt had pulled up slightly on one side, showing clean white skin. I looked at it and began to get an extremely useless and uncomfortable erection.

I tried to divert my mind to a new track and got thinking about how I had wanted to paint Brent Norton yesterday. No, nothing as important as a painting, but . . . just sit him on a log with my beer in his hand and sketch his sweaty, tired face and the two wings of his carefully processed hair sticking up untidily in the back. It could have been a good picture. It took me twenty years of living with my father to accept the idea that being good could be good enough.

You know what talent is? The curse of expectation. As a kid you have to deal with that, beat it somehow. If you can write, you think God put you on earth to blow Shakespeare away. Or if you can paint, maybe you think—I did—that God put you on earth to blow your father away.

It turned out I wasn't as good as he was. I kept trying to be for longer than I should have, maybe. I had a show in New York and it did poorly—the art critics beat me over the head with my father. A year later I was supporting myself and Steff with the commercial stuff. She was pregnant and I sat down and talked to myself about it. The result of that conversation was a belief that serious art was always going to be a hobby for me, no more.

I did Golden Girl Shampoo ads—the one where the Girl is standing astride her bike, the one where she's playing Frisbee on the beach, the one where she's standing on the balcony of her apartment with a drink in her hand. I've done short-story illustrations for most of the big slicks, but I broke into that field doing fast illustrations for the stories in the sleazier men's magazines. I've done some movie posters. The money comes in. We keep our heads nicely above water.

I had one final show in Bridgton, just last summer. I showed nine canvases that I had painted in five years, and I sold six of them. The one I absolutely would not sell showed the Federal market, by some queer coincidence. The perspective was from the far end of the parking lot. In my picture, the parking lot was empty except for a line of Campbell's Beans and Franks cans, each one larger than the last as they marched toward the viewer's eye. The last one appeared to be about eight feet tall. The picture was titled *Beans and False Perspective*. A man from California who was a top exec in some company that makes tennis balls and rackets and who knows what other sports equipment seemed to want that picture very badly, and would not take no for an answer in spite of the NFS card tucked into the bottom left-hand corner of the spare wooden frame. He began at six hundred dollars and worked his way up to four thousand. He said he wanted it for his study. I would not let him have it, and he went away sorely puzzled. Even so, he didn't quite give up; he left his card in case I changed my mind.

I could have used the money—that was the year we put the addition on the house and bought the four-wheel-drive—but I just couldn't sell it. I couldn't sell it because I felt it was the best painting I had ever done and I wanted it to look at after someone would ask me, with totally unconscious cruelty, when I was going to do something serious.

Then I happened to show it to Ollie Weeks one day last fall. He asked me if he could photograph it and run it as an ad one week, and that was the end of my own false perspective. Ollie had recognized my painting for what it was, and by doing so, he forced me to recognize it, too. A perfectly good piece of slick commercial art. No more. And, thank God, no less.

I let him do it, and then I called the exec at his home in San Luis Obispo and told him he could have the painting for twenty-five hundred if he still wanted it. He did, and I shipped it UPS to the coast. And since then that voice of disappointed expectation—that cheated child's voice that can never be satisfied with such a mild superlative as good—has fallen pretty much silent. And except for a few rumbles—like the sounds of those unseen creatures somewhere out in the foggy night—it has been pretty much silent ever since. Maybe you can tell me—why should the silencing of that childish, demanding voice seem so much like dying?

Around four o'clock Billy woke up—partially, at least—and looked around with bleary, uncomprehending eyes. "Are we still here?"

"Yeah, honey," I said. "We are."

He started to cry with a weak helplessness that was horrible. Amanda woke up and looked at us.

"Hey, kid," she said, and pulled him gently to her. "Everything is going to look a little better come morning."

"No," Billy said. "No it won't. It won't. It won't."

"Shh," she said. Her eyes met mine over his head. "Shh, it's past your bedtime."

"I want my *mother!*"

"Yeah, you do," Amanda said. "Of course you do."

Billy squirmed around in her lap until he could look at me. Which he did for some time. And then slept again.

"Thanks," I said. "He needed you."

"He doesn't even know me."

"That doesn't change it."

"So what do you think?" she asked. Her green eyes held mine steadily. "What do you really think?"

"Ask me in the morning."

"I'm asking you now."

I opened my mouth to answer and then Ollie Weeks materialized out of the gloom like something from a horror tale. He had a flashlight with one of the ladies' blouses over the lens, and he was pointing it toward the ceiling. It made strange shadows on his haggard face. "David," he whispered.

Amanda looked at him, first startled, then scared again.

"Ollie, what is it?" I asked.

"David," he whispered again. Then: "Come on. Please."

"I don't want to leave Billy. He just went to sleep."

"I'll be with him," Amanda said. "You better go." Then, in a lower voice: "Jesus, this is never going to end."

VIII

What Happened to
the Soldiers.
With Amanda.
A Conversation with
Dan Miller.

I went with Ollie. He was headed for the storage area. As we passed the cooler, he grabbed a beer.

"Ollie, what is it?"

"I want you to see it."

He pushed through the double doors. They slipped shut behind us with a little backwash of air. It was cold. I didn't like this place, not after what had happened to Norm. A part of my mind insisted on reminding me that there was still a small scrap of dead tentacle lying around someplace.

Ollie let the blouse drop from the lens of his light. He trained it overhead. At first I had an idea that someone had hung a couple of mannequins from one of the heating pipes below the ceiling. That they had hung them on piano wire or something, a kid's Halloween trick.

Then I noticed the feet, dangling about seven inches off the cement floor. There were two piles of kicked-over cartons. I looked up at the faces and a scream began to rise in my throat because they were not the faces of department-store dummies. Both heads were cocked to the side, as if appreciating some horribly funny joke, a joke that had made them laugh until they turned purple.

Their shadows. Their shadows thrown long on the wall behind them. Their tongues. Their protruding tongues.

They were both wearing uniforms. They were the kids I had noticed earlier and had lost track of along the way. The army brats from—

The scream. I could hear it starting in my throat as a moan, rising like a police siren, and then Ollie gripped my arm just above the elbow. "Don't scream, David. No one knows about this but you and me. And that's how I want to keep it."

Somehow I bit it back.

"Those army kids," I managed.

"From the Arrowhead Project," Ollie said. "Sure." Something cold was thrust into my hand. The beer can. "Drink this. You need it."

I drained the can completely dry.

Ollie said, "I came back to see if we had any extra cartridges for that gas grill Mr. McVey has been using. I saw these guys. The way I figure, they must have gotten the nooses ready and stood on top of those two piles of cartons. They must have tied their hands for each other and then balanced each other while they stepped through the length of rope between their wrists. So . . . so that their hands would be behind them, you know. Then—this is the way I figure—they stuck their heads into the nooses and pulled them tight by jerking their heads to one side. Maybe one of them counted to three and they jumped together. I don't know.''

"It couldn't be done," I said through a dry mouth. But their hands were tied behind them, all right. I couldn't seem to take my eyes away from that.

"It could. If they wanted to bad enough, David, they could."

"But why?"

"I think you know why. Not any of the tourists, the summer people—like that guy Miller—but there are people from around here who could make a pretty decent guess."

"The Arrowhead Project?"

Ollie said, "I stand by one of those registers all day long and I hear a lot. All this spring I've been hearing things about that damned Arrowhead thing, none of it good. The black ice on the lakes—"

I thought of Bill Giosti leaning in my window, blowing warm alcohol in my face. Not just atoms, but *different* atoms. Now these bodies hanging from that overhead pipe. The cocked heads. The dangling shoes. The tongues protruding like summer sausages.

I realized with fresh horror that new doors of perception were opening up inside. New? Not so. Old doors of perception. The perception of a child who has not yet learned to protect itself by developing the tunnel vision that keeps out ninety percent of the universe. Children see everything their eyes happen upon, hear everything in their ears' range. But if life is the rise of consciousness (as a crewel-work sampler my wife made in high school proclaims), then it is also the reduction of input.

Terror is the widening of perspective and perception. The horror was in knowing I was swimming down to a place most of us leave when we get out of diapers and into training pants. I could see it on Ollie's face, too. When rationality begins to break down, the circuits of the human brain can overload. Axons grow bright and feverish. Hallucinations turn real: the quicksilver puddle at the point where perspective makes parallel lines seem to intersect is really there; the dead walk and talk; a rose begins to sing.

"I've heard stuff from maybe two dozen people," Ollie said. "Justine Robards. Nick Tochai. Ben Michaelson. You can't keep secrets in small towns. Things get out. Sometimes it's like a spring—it just bubbles up out of the earth and no one has an idea where it came from. You overhear something at the library and pass it on, or at the marina in Harrison, Christ knows where else, or why. But all spring and summer I've been hearing Arrowhead Project, Arrowhead Project."

"But these two," I said. "Christ, Ollie, they're just kids."

"There were kids in Nam who used to take ears. I was there. I saw it."

"But . . . what would drive them to do this?"

"I don't know. Maybe they knew something.

Maybe they only suspected. They must have known people in here would start asking them questions eventually. If there is an eventually."

"If you're right," I said, "it must be something really bad."

"That storm," Ollie said in his soft, level voice. "Maybe it knocked something loose up there. Maybe there was an accident. They could have been fooling around with anything. Some people claim they were messing with high-intensity lasers and masers. Sometimes I hear fusion power. And suppose . . . suppose they ripped a hole straight through into another dimension?"

"That's hogwash," I said.

"Are they?" Ollie asked, and pointed at the bodies.

"No. The question now is: What do we do?"

"I think we ought to cut them down and hide them," he said promptly. "Put them under a pile of stuff people won't want—dog food, dish detergent, stuff like that. If this gets out, it will only make things worse. That's why I came to you, David. I felt you are the only one I could really trust."

I muttered, "It's like the Nazi war criminals killing themselves in their cells after the war was lost."

"Yeah. I had that same thought."

We fell silent, and suddenly those soft shuffling noises began outside the steel loading door again— the sound of the tentacles feeling softly across it. We drew together. My flesh was crawling.

"Okay," I said.

"We'll make it as quick as we can," Ollie said. His sapphire ring glowed mutely as he moved his flashlight. "I want to get out of here fast."

I looked up at the ropes. They had used the same sort of clothesline the man in the golf cap had allowed me to tie around his waist. The nooses had sunk into the puffed flesh of their necks, and I wondered again what it could have been to make both of them go through with it. I knew what Ollie meant by saying that if the news of the double suicide got out, it would make things worse. For me it already had—and I wouldn't have believed that possible.

There was a snicking sound. Ollie had opened his knife, a good heavy job made for slitting open cartons. And, of course, cutting rope.

"You or me?" he asked.

I swallowed. "One each."

We did it.

When I got back, Amanda was gone and Mrs. Turman was with Billy. They were both sleeping. I walked down one of the aisles and a voice said: "Mr. Drayton. David." It was Amanda, standing by the stairs to the manager's office, her eyes like emeralds. "What was it?"

"Nothing," I said.

She came over to me. I could smell faint perfume. And oh how I wanted her. "You liar," she said.

"It was nothing. A false alarm."

"If that's how you want it." She took my hand. "I've just been up to the office. It's empty and there's a lock on the door." Her face was perfectly calm, but her eyes were lambent, almost feral, and a pulse beat steadily in her throat.

"I don't—"

"I saw the way you looked at me," she said. "If we need to talk about it, it's no good. The Turman woman is with your son."

"Yes." It came to me that this was a way—maybe not the best one, but a way, nevertheless—to take the curse off what Ollie and I had just done. Not the best way, just the only way.

We went up the narrow flight of stairs and into the office. It was empty, as she had said. And there was a lock on the door. I turned it. In the darkness she was nothing but a shape. I put my arms out, touched her, and pulled her to me. She was trembling. We went down on the floor, first kneeling, kissing, and I cupped one firm breast and could feel the quick thudding of her heart through her sweatshirt. I thought of Steffy telling Billy not to touch the live wires. I thought of the bruise that had been on her hip when she took off the brown dress on our wedding night. I thought of the first time I had seen her, biking across the mall of the University of Maine at Orono, me bound for one of Vincent Hartgen's classes with my portfolio under my arm. And my erection was enormous.

We lay down then, and she said, "Love me, David. Make me warm." When she came, she dug into my back with her nails and called me by a name that wasn't mine. I didn't mind. It made us about even.

When we came down, some sort of creeping dawn had begun. The blackness outside the loopholes went reluctantly to dull gray, then to chrome, then to the bright, featureless, and unsparkling white of a drive-in movie screen. Mike Hatlen was asleep in a folding chair he had scrounged somewhere. Dan Miller sat on the floor a little distance away, eating a Hostess donut. The kind that's powdered with white sugar.

"Sit down, Mr. Drayton," he invited.

I looked around for Amanda, but she was already halfway up the aisle. She didn't look back. Our act of love in the dark already seemed something out of a fantasy, impossible to believe even in this weird daylight. I sat down.

"Have a donut." He held the box out.

I shook my head. "All that white sugar is death. Worse than cigarettes."

That made him laugh a little bit. "In that case, have two."

I was surprised to find a little laughter left inside me—he had surprised it out, and I liked him for it. I did take two of his donuts. They tasted pretty good. I chased them with a cigarette, although it is not normally my habit to smoke in the mornings.

"I ought to get back to my kid," I said. "He'll be waking up."

Miller nodded. "Those pink bugs," he said. "They're all gone. So are the birds. Hank Vannerman said the last one hit the windows around four. Apparently the . . . the wildlife . . . is a lot more active when it's dark."

"You don't want to tell Brent Norton that," I said. "Or Norm."

He nodded again and didn't say anything for a long time. Then he lit a cigarette of his own and looked at me. "We can't stay here, Drayton," he said.

"There's food. Plenty to drink."

"The supplies don't have anything to do with it, and you know it. What do we do if one of the big beasties out there decides to break in instead of just going bump in the night? Do we try to drive it off with broom handles and charcoal lighter fluid?"

Of course he was right. Perhaps the mist was protecting us in a way. Hiding us. But maybe it wouldn't hide us for long, and there was more to it than that. We had been in the Federal for eighteen hours, more or less, and I could feel a kind of lethargy spreading over me, not much different from the lethargy I've felt on one or two occasions when I've tried to swim too far. There was an urge to play it safe, to just stay put, to take care of Billy (*and maybe to bang Amanda Dumfries in the middle of the night*, a voice murmured), to see if the mist wouldn't just lift, leaving everything as it had been.

I could see it on the other faces as well, and it suddenly occurred to me that there were people now in the Federal who probably wouldn't leave under any circumstance. The very thought of going out the door after all that had happened would freeze them.

Miller had been watching these thoughts cross my face, maybe. He said, "There were about eighty people in here when that damn fog came. From that number you subtract the bag-boy, Norton, and the four people that went out with him, and that man Smalley. That leaves seventy-three.''

And subtracting the two soldiers, now resting under a stack of Purina Puppy Chow bags, it made seventy-one.

''Then you subtract the people who have just opted out,'' he went on. ''There are ten or twelve of those. Say ten. That leaves about sixty-three. *But—*'' He raised one sugar-powdered finger. ''Of those sixty-three, we've got twenty or so that just won't leave. You'd have to drag them out kicking and screaming.''

''Which all goes to prove what?''

''That we've got to get out, that's all. And I'm going. Around noon, I think. I'm planning to take as many people as will come. I'd like you and your boy to come along.''

''After what happened to Norton?''

''Norton went like a lamb to the slaughter. That doesn't mean I have to, or the people who come with me.''

''How can you prevent it? We have exactly one gun.''

''And lucky to have that. But if we could make it across the intersection, maybe we could get down to the Sportsman's Exchange on Main Street. They've got more guns there than you could shake a stick at.''

''That's one 'if' and one 'maybe' too many.''

''Drayton,'' he said, ''it's an iffy situation.''

That rolled very smoothly off his tongue, but he didn't have a little boy to watch out for.

"Look, let it pass for now, okay? I didn't get much sleep last night, but I got a chance to think over a few things. Want to hear them?"

"Sure."

He stood up and stretched. "Take a walk over to the window with me."

We went through the checkout lane nearest the bread racks and stood at one of the loopholes. The man who was keeping watch there said, "The bugs are gone."

Miller slapped him on the back. "Go get yourself a coffee—and, fella, I'll keep an eye out."

"Okay. Thanks."

He walked away, and Miller and I stepped up to his loophole. "So tell me what you see out there," he said.

I looked. The litter barrel had been knocked over in the night, probably by one of the swooping bird-things, spilling a trash of papers, cans, and paper shake cups from the Dairy Queen down the road all over the hottop. Beyond that I could see the rank of cars closest to the market fading into whiteness. That was all I could see, and I told him so.

"That blue Chevy pickup is mine," he said. He pointed and I could see just a hint of blue in the mist. "But if you think back to when you pulled in yesterday, you'll remember that the parking lot was pretty jammed, right?"

I glanced back at my Scout and remembered I had only gotten the space close to the market because someone else had been pulling out. I nodded.

Miller said, "Now couple something else with that fact, Drayton. Norton and his four . . . what did you call them?"

"Flat-Earthers."

"Yeah, that's good. Just what they were. They go out, right? Almost the full length of that clothesline. Then we heard those roaring noises, like there was a goddamn herd of elephants out there. Right?"

"It didn't sound like elephants," I said. "It sounded like—" *Like something from the primordial ooze* was the phrase that came to mind, but I didn't want to say that to Miller, not after he had clapped that guy on the back and told him to go get a coffee-and like the coach jerking a player from the big game. I might have said it to Ollie, but not to Miller. "I don't know what it sounded like," I finished lamely.

"But it sounded *big*."

"Yeah." It had sounded pretty goddamn big.

"So how come we didn't hear cars getting bashed around? Screeching metal? Breaking glass?"

"Well, because—" I stopped. He had me. "I don't know."

Miller said, "No way they were out of the parking lot when whatever-it-was hit them. I'll tell you what I think. I think we didn't hear any cars getting around because a lot of them might be gone. Just . . . gone. Fallen into the earth, vaporized, you name it. Strong enough to splinter these beams and twist them out of shape and knock stuff off the shelves. And the town whistle stopped at the same time."

I was trying to visualize half the parking lot gone. Trying to visualize walking out there and just coming to a brand-new drop in the land where the hottop with its neat yellow-lined parking slots left off. A drop, a slope . . . or maybe an out-and-out precipice falling away into the featureless white mist . . .

After a couple of seconds I said, "If you're right, how far do you think you're going to get in your pickup?"

"I wasn't thinking of my truck. I was thinking of your four-wheel-drive."

That was something to chew over, but not now. "What else is on your mind?"

Miller was eager to go on. "The pharmacy next door, that's on my mind. What about that?"

I opened my mouth to say I didn't have the slightest idea what he was talking about, and then shut it with a snap. The Bridgton Pharmacy had been doing business when we drove in yesterday. Not the Laundromat, but the drugstore had been wide open, the doors chocked with rubber doorstops to let in a little cool air—the power outage had killed their air-conditioning, of course. The door to the pharmacy could be no more than twenty feet from the door of the Federal market. So why—

"Why haven't any of those people turned up over here?" Miller asked for me. "It's been eighteen hours. Aren't they hungry? They're sure not over there eating Dristan and Stayfree Mini-pads."

"There's food," I said. "They're always selling food items on special. Sometimes it's animal crackers, sometimes it's those toaster pastries, all sorts of things. Plus the candy rack."

"I just don't believe they'd stick with stuff like that when there's all kinds of stuff over here."

"What are you getting at?"

"What I'm getting at is that I want to get out but I don't want to be dinner for some refugee from a grade-B horror picture. Four or five of us could go next door and check out the situation in the drugstore. As sort of a trial balloon."

"That's everything?"

"No, there's one other thing."

"What's that?"

"Her," Miller said simply, and jerked his thumb toward one of the middle aisles. "That crazy cunt. That witch."

It was Mrs. Carmody he had jerked his thumb at. She was no longer alone; two women had joined her. From their bright clothes I guessed they were probably tourists or summer people, ladies who had maybe left their families to "just run into town and get a few things" and were now eaten up with worry over their husbands and kids. Ladies eager to grasp at almost any straw. Maybe even the black comfort of a Mrs. Carmody.

Her pantsuit shone out with its same baleful resplendence. She was talking, gesturing, her face hard and grim. The two ladies in their bright clothes (but not as bright as Mrs. Carmody's pantsuit, no, and her gigantic satchel of a purse was still tucked firmly under one doughy arm) were listening raptly.

"She's another reason I want to get out, Drayton. By tonight she'll have six people sitting with her. If those pink bugs and the birds come back tonight, she'll have a whole congregation sitting with her by tomorrow morning. Then we can start worrying about who she'll tell them to sacrifice to make it all better. Maybe me, or you, or that guy Hatlen. Maybe your kid."

"That's idiocy," I said. But was it? The cold chill crawling up my back said not necessarily. Mrs. Carmody's mouth moved and moved. The eyes of the tourist ladies were fixed on her wrinkled lips. Was it idiocy? I thought of the dusty stuffed animals drinking at their looking-glass stream. Mrs. Carmody had power. Even Steff, normally hardheaded and straight-from-the-shoulder, invoked the old lady's name with unease.

That crazy cunt, Miller had called her. *That witch.*

"The people in this market are going through a section-eight experience for sure," Miller said. He gestured at the red-painted beams framing the show-window segments . . . twisted and splintered and buckled out of shape. "Their minds probably feel like those beams look. Mine sure as shit does. I spent half of last night thinking I must have flipped out of my gourd, that I was probably in a straitjacket in Danvers, raving my head off about bugs and dinosaur birds and tentacles and that it would all go away just as soon as the nice orderly came along and shot a wad of Thorazine into my arm." His small face was strained and white. He looked at Mrs. Carmody and then back at me. "I tell you it might happen. As people get flakier, she's going to look better and better to some of them. And I don't want to be around if that happens."

Mrs. Carmody's lips, moving and moving. Her tongue dancing around her old lady's snaggle teeth. She did look like a witch. Put her in a pointy black hat and she would be perfect. What was she saying to her two captured birds in their bright summer plumage?

Arrowhead Project? Black Spring? Abominations from the cellars of the earth? Human sacrifice?

Bullshit.

All the same—

"So what do you say?"

"I'll go this far," I answered him. "We'll try going over to the drug. You, me, Ollie if he wants to go, one or two others. Then we'll talk it over again." Even that gave me the feeling of walking out over an impossible drop on a narrow beam. I wasn't going to help Billy by killing myself. On the other hand, I wasn't going to help him by just sitting on my ass, either. Twenty feet to the drugstore. That wasn't so bad.

"When?" he asked.

"Give me an hour."

"Sure," he said.

IX

The Expedition to the Pharmacy.

I told Mrs. Turman, and I told Amanda, and then I told Billy. He seemed better this morning; he had eaten two donuts and a bowl of Special K for breakfast. Afterward I raced him up and down two of the aisles and even got him giggling a little. Kids are so adaptable that they can scare the living shit right out of you. He was too pale, the flesh under his eyes was still puffed from the tears he had cried in the night, and his face had a horribly *used* look. In a way it had become like an old man's face, as if too much emotional voltage had been running behind it for too long. But he was still alive and still able to laugh . . . at least until he remembered where he was and what was happening.

After the windsprints we sat down with Amanda and Hattie Turman and drank Gatorade from paper cups and I told him I was going over to the drugstore with a few other people.

"I don't want you to," he said immediately, his face clouding.

"It'll be all right, Big Bill. I'll bring you a *Spider-Man* comic book."

"I want you to stay *here*." Now his face was not just cloudy; it was thundery. I took his hand. He pulled it away. I took it again.

"Billy, we have to get out of here sooner or later. You see that, don't you?"

"When the fog goes away . . ." But he spoke with no conviction at all. He drank his Gatorade slowly and without relish.

"Billy, it's been almost one whole day now."

"I want Mommy."

"Well, maybe this is the first step on the way to getting back to her."

Mrs. Turman said, "Don't build the boy's hopes up, David."

"What the hell," I snapped at her, "the kid's got to hope for something."

She dropped her eyes. "Yes. I suppose he does."

Billy took no notice of this. "Daddy . . . Daddy, there are things out there. *Things.*"

"Yes, we know that. But a lot of them—not all, but a lot—don't seem to come out until it's nighttime."

"They'll wait," he said. His eyes were huge, centered on mine. "They'll wait in the fog . . . and when you can't get back inside, they'll come to eat you up. Like in the fairy stories." He hugged me with fierce, panicky tightness. "Daddy, please don't go."

I pried his arms loose as gently as I could and told him that I had to. "But I'll be back, Billy."

"All right," he said huskily, but he wouldn't look at me anymore. He didn't believe I would be back. It was on his face, which was no longer thundery but woeful and grieving. I wondered again if I could be doing the right thing, putting myself at risk. Then I happened to glance down the middle aisle and saw Mrs. Carmody there. She had gained a third listener, a man with a grizzled cheek and a mean and rolling bloodshot eye. His haggard brow and shaking hands almost screamed the word hangover. It was none other than your friend and his, Myron LaFleur. The fellow who had felt no compunction at all about sending a boy out to do a man's job.

That crazy cunt. That witch.

I kissed Billy and hugged him hard. Then I walked down to the front of the store—but not down the housewares aisle. I didn't want to fall under her eye.

Three-quarters of the way down, Amanda caught up with me. "Do you really have to do this?" she asked.

"Yes, I think so."

"Forgive me if I say it sounds like so much macho bullshit to me." There were spots of color high on her cheeks and her eyes were greener than ever. She was highly—no, royally—pissed.

I took her arm and recapped my discussion with Dan Miller. The riddle of the cars and the fact that no one from the pharmacy had joined us didn't move her much. The business about Mrs. Carmody did.

"He could be right," she said.

"Do you really believe that?"

"I don't know. There's a poisonous feel to that woman. And if people are frightened badly enough for long enough, they'll turn to anyone that promises a solution."

"But human sacrifice, Amanda?"

"The Aztecs were into it," she said evenly. "Listen, David. You come back. If anything happens . . . *anything* . . . you come back. Cut and run if you have to. Not for me, what happened last night was nice, but that was last night. Come back for your boy."

"Yes. I will."

"I wonder," she said, and now she looked like Billy, haggard and old. It occurred to me that most of us looked that way. But not Mrs. Carmody. Mrs. Carmody looked younger somehow, and more vital. As if she had come into her own. As if . . . as if she were thriving on it.

We didn't get going until 9:30 A.M. Seven of us went: Ollie, Dan Miller, Mike Hatlen, Myron LaFleur's erstwhile buddy Jim (also hungover, but seemingly determined to find some way to atone), Buddy Eagleton, myself. The seventh was Hilda Reppler. Miller and Hatlen tried halfheartedly to talk her out of coming. She would have none of it. I didn't even try. I suspected she might be more competent than any of us, except maybe for Ollie. She was carrying a small canvas shopping basket, and it was loaded with an arsenal of Raid and Black Flag spray cans, all of them uncapped and ready for action. In her free hand she held a Spaulding Jimmy Connors tennis racket from a display of sporting goods in Aisle 2.

"What you gonna do with that, Mrs. Reppler?" Jim asked.

"I don't know," she said. She had a low, raspy, competent voice. "But it feels right in my hand." She looked him over closely, and her eye was cold. "Jim Grondin, isn't it? Didn't I have you in school?"

Jim's lips stretched in an uneasy egg-suck grin. "Yes'm. Me and my sister Pauline."

"Too much to drink last night?"

Jim, who towered over her and probably out-weighed her by one hundred pounds, blushed to the roots of his American Legion crewcut. "Aw, no—"

She turned away curtly, cutting him off. "I think we're ready," she said.

All of us had something, although you would have called it an odd assortment of weapons. Ollie had Amanda's gun, Buddy Eagleton had a steel pinchbar from out back somewhere. I had a broom handle.

"Okay," Dan Miller said, raising his voice a bit. "You folks want to listen up a minute?"

A dozen people had drifted down toward the OUT door to see what was going on. They were loosely knotted, and to their right stood Mrs. Carmody and her new friends.

"We're going over to the drugstore to see what the situation is there. Hopefully, we'll be able to bring something back to aid Mrs. Clapham." She was the lady who had been trampled yesterday, when the bugs came. One of her legs had been broken and she was in a great deal of pain.

Miller looked us over. "We're not going to take any chances," he said. "At the first sign of anything threatening, we're going to pop back into the market—"

"And bring all the fiends of hell down on our heads!" Mrs. Carmody cried.

"She's right!" one of the summer ladies seconded. "You'll make them notice us! You'll make them come! Why can't you just leave well enough alone?"

There was a murmur of agreement from some of the people who had gathered to watch us go.

I said, "Lady, is this what you call well enough?"

She dropped her eyes, confused.

Mrs. Carmody marched a step forward. Her eyes were blazing. "You'll die out there, David Drayton! Do you want to make your son an orphan?" She raised her eyes and raked all of us with them. Buddy Eagleton dropped his eyes and simultaneously raised the pinchbar, as if to ward her off.

"All of you will die out there! Haven't you realized that the end of the world has come? The Fiend has been let loose! Star Wormwood blazes and each one of you that steps out that door will be torn apart! And they'll come for those of us who are left, just as this good woman said! Are you people going to let that happen?" She was appealing to the onlookers now, and a little mutter ran through them. "After what happened to the unbelievers yesterday? It's death! *It's death! It's—*"

A can of peas flew across two of the checkout lanes suddenly and struck Mrs. Carmody on the right breast. She staggered backward with a startled squawk.

Amanda stood forward. "Shut up," she said. "Shut up, you miserable buzzard."

"She serves the Foul One!" Mrs. Carmody screamed. A jittery smile hung on her face. "Who did you sleep with last night, missus? Who did you lie down with last night? Mother Carmody sees, oh yes, Mother Carmody sees what others miss."

But the moment's spell she had created was broken, and Amanda's eyes never wavered.

"Are we going or are we going to stand here all day?" Mrs. Reppler asked.

And we went. God help us, we went.

Dan Miller was in the lead. Ollie came second, I was last, with Mrs. Reppler in front of me. I was as scared as I've ever been, I think, and the hand wrapped around my broom handle was sweaty-slick.

There was that thin, acrid, and unnatural smell of the mist. By the time I got out the door, Miller and Ollie had already faded into it, and Hatlen, who was third, was nearly out of sight.

Only twenty feet, I kept telling myself. *Only twenty feet.*

Mrs. Reppler walked slowly and firmly ahead of me, her tennis racket swinging lightly from her right hand. To our left was a red cinderblock wall. To our right the first rank of cars, looming out of the mist like ghost ships. Another trash barrel materialized out of the whiteness, and beyond that was a bench where people sometimes sat to wait their turn at the pay phone. *Only twenty feet, Miller's probably there by now, twenty feet is only ten or twelve paces, so—*

"Oh my God!" Miller screamed. "Oh dear sweet God, look at this!"

Miller had gotten there, all right.

Buddy Eagleton was ahead of Mrs. Reppler and he turned to run, his eyes wide and stary. She batted him lightly in the chest with her tennis racket. "Where do you think *you're* going?" she asked in her tough, slightly raspy voice, and that was all the panic there was.

The rest of us drew up to Miller. I took one glance back over my shoulder and saw that the Federal had been swallowed by the mist. The red cinderblock wall faded to a thin wash pink and then disappeared utterly, probably five feet on the Bridgton Pharmacy side of the OUT door. I felt more isolated, more simply alone, than ever in my life. It was as if I had lost the womb.

The pharmacy had been the scene of a slaughter.

Miller and I, of course, were very close to it— almost on top of it. All the things in the mist operated primarily by sense of smell. It stood to reason. Sight would have been almost completely useless to them. Hearing a little better, but as I've said, the mist had a way of screwing up the acoustics, making things that were close sound distant and— sometimes—things that were far away sound close.

The things in the mist followed their truest sense. They followed their noses.

Those of us in the market had been saved by the power outage as much as by anything else. The electric-eye doors wouldn't operate. In a sense, the market had been sealed up when the mist came. But the pharmacy doors . . . they had been chocked open. The power failure had killed their air-conditioning and they had opened the doors to let in the breeze. Only something else had come in as well.

A man in a maroon T-shirt lay facedown in the doorway. Or at first I thought his T-shirt was maroon; then I saw a few white patches at the bottom and understood that once it had been all white. The maroon was dried blood. And there was something else wrong with him. I puzzled it over in my mind. Even when Buddy Eagleton turned around and was noisily sick, it didn't come immediately. I guess when something that . . . that *final* happens to someone, your mind rejects it at first . . . unless maybe you're in a war.

His head was gone, that's what it was. His legs were splayed out inside the pharmacy doors, and his head should have been hanging over the low step. But his head just wasn't.

Jim Grondin had had enough. He turned away, his hands over his mouth, his bloodshot eyes gazing madly into mine. Then he stumbled-staggered back toward the market.

The others took no notice. Miller had stepped inside. Mike Hatlen followed. Mrs. Reppler stationed herself at one side of the double doors with her tennis racket. Ollie stood on the other side with Amanda's gun drawn and pointing at the pavement.

He said quietly, "I seem to be running out of hope, David."

Buddy Eagleton was leaning weakly against the pay-phone stall like someone who has just gotten bad news from home. His broad shoulders shook with the force of his sobs.

"Don't count us out yet," I said to Ollie. I stepped up to the door. I didn't want to go inside, but I had promised my son a comic book.

The Bridgton Pharmacy was a crazy shambles. Paperbacks and magazines were everywhere. There was a *Spider-Man* comic and an *Incredible Hulk* almost at my feet, and without thinking, I picked them up and jammed them into my back pocket for Billy. Bottles and boxes lay in the aisles. A hand hung over one of the racks.

Unreality washed over me. The wreckage . . . the *carnage*—that was bad enough. But the place also looked like it had been the scene of some crazy party. It was hung and festooned with what I at first took to be streamers. But they weren't broad and flat; they were more like very thick strings or very thin cables. It struck me that they were almost the same bright white as the mist itself, and a cold chill sketched its way up my back like frost. Not crepe. What? Magazines and books hung dangling in the air from some of them.

Mike Hatlen was prodding a strange black thing with one foot. It was long and bristly. "What the fuck is this?" he asked no one in particular.

And suddenly I knew. I knew what had killed all those unlucky enough to be in the pharmacy when the mist came. The people who had been unlucky enough to get smelled out. *Out—*

"Out," I said. My throat was completely dry, and the word came out like a lint-covered bullet. "Get out of here."

Ollie looked at me. "David . . . ?"

"They're spiderwebs," I said. And then two screams came out of the mist. The first of fear, maybe. The second of pain. It was Jim. If there were dues to be paid, he was paying them.

"Get out!" I shouted at Mike and Dan Miller.

Then something looped out of the mist. It was impossible to see it against that white background, but I could hear it. It sounded like a bullwhip that had been halfheartedly flicked. And I could see it when it twisted around the thigh of Buddy Eagleton's jeans.

He screamed and grabbed for the first thing handy, which happened to be the telephone. The handset flew the length of its cord and then swung back and forth. *"Oh Jesus that HURTS!"* Buddy screamed.

Ollie grabbed for him, and I saw what was happening. At the same instant I understood why the head of the man in the doorway was missing. The thin white cable that had twisted around Buddy's leg like a silk rope *was sinking into his flesh.* That leg of his jeans had been neatly cut off and was sliding down his leg. A neat, circular incision in his flesh was brimming blood as the cable went deeper.

Ollie pulled him hard. There was a thin snapping sound and Buddy was free. His lips had gone blue with shock.

Mike and Dan were coming, but too slowly. Then Dan ran into several hanging threads and got stuck, exactly like a bug on flypaper. He freed himself with a tremendous jerk, leaving a flap of his shirt hanging from the webbing.

Suddenly the air was full of those languorous bull-whip cracks, and the thin white cables were drifting down all around us. They were coated with the same corrosive substance. I dodged two of them, more by luck than by skill. One landed at my feet and I could hear a faint hiss of bubbling hottop. Another floated out of the air and Mrs. Reppler calmly swung her tennis racket at it. The thread stuck fast, and I heard a high-pitched *twing! twing! twing!* as the corrosive ate through the racket's strings and snapped them. It sounded like someone rapidly plucking the strings of a violin. A moment later a thread wrapped around the upper handle of the racket and it was jerked into the mist.

"Get back!" Ollie screamed.

We got moving. Ollie had an arm around Buddy. Dan Miller and Mike Hatlen were on each side of Mrs. Reppler. The white strands of web continued to drift out of the fog, impossible to see unless your eye could pick them out against the red cinderblock background.

One of them wrapped around Mike Hatlen's left arm. Another whipped around his neck in a series of quick winding-up snaps. His jugular went in a jetting, jumping explosion and he was dragged away, head lolling. One of his Bass loafers fell off and lay there on its side.

Buddy suddenly slumped forward, almost dragging Ollie to his knees. "He's passed out, David. Help me."

I grabbed Buddy around the waist and we pulled him along in a clumsy, stumbling fashion. Even in unconsciousness, Buddy kept his grip on his steel pinchbar. The leg that the strand of web had wrapped around hung away from his body at a terrible angle.

Mrs. Reppler had turned around. "Ware!" she screamed in her rusty voice. "Ware behind you!"

As I started to turn, one of the web-strands floated down on top of Dan Miller's head. His hands beat at it, tore at it.

One of the spiders had come out of the mist from behind us. It was the size of a big dog. It was black with yellow piping. *Racing stripes*, I thought crazily. Its eyes were reddish-purple, like pomegranates. It strutted busily toward us on what might have been as many as twelve or fourteen many-jointed legs—it was no ordinary earthly spider blown up to horror-movie size; it was something totally different, perhaps not really a spider at all. Seeing it, Mike Hatlen would have understood what that bristly black thing he had been prodding at in the pharmacy really was.

It closed in on us, spinning its webbing from an oval-shaped orifice on its upper belly. The strands floated out toward us in what was nearly a fan shape. Looking at this nightmare, so like the death-black spiders brooding over their dead flies and bugs in the shadows of our boathouse, I felt my mind trying to tear completely loose from its moorings. I believe now that it was only the thought of Billy that allowed me to keep any semblance of sanity. I was making some sound. Laughing. Crying. Screaming. I don't know.

But Ollie Weeks was like a rock. He raised Amanda's pistol as calmly as a man on a target range and emptied it in spaced shots into the creature at point-blank range. Whatever hell it came from, it wasn't invulnerable. A black ichor splattered from its body and it made a terrible mewling sound, so low it was more felt than heard, like a bass note from a synthesizer. Then it scuttered back into the mist and was gone. It might have been a phantasm from a horrible drug-dream . . . except for the puddles of sticky black stuff it had left behind.

There was a clang as Buddy finally dropped his steel pinchbar.

"He's dead," Ollie said. "Let him go, David. The fucking thing got his femoral artery, he's dead. Let's get the Christ out of here." His face was once more running with sweat and his eyes bulged from his big round face. One of the web-strands floated easily down on the back of his hand and Ollie swung his arm, snapping it. The strand left a bloody weal.

Mrs. Reppler screamed "Ware!" again, and we turned toward her. Another of them had come out of the mist and had wrapped its legs around Dan Miller in a mad lover's embrace. He was striking at it with his fists. As I bent and picked up Buddy's pinchbar, the spider began to wrap Dan in its deadly thread, and his struggles became a grisly, jittering death dance.

Mrs. Reppler walked toward the spider with a can of Black Flag insect repellent held outstretched in one hand. The spider's legs reached for her. She depressed the button and a cloud of the stuff jetted into one of its sparkling jewellike eyes. That low-pitched mewling sound came again. The spider seemed to shudder all over and then it began to lurch backward, hairy legs scratching at the pavement. It dragged Dan's body, bumping and rolling, behind it. Mrs. Reppler threw the can of bug spray at it. It bounced off the spider's body and clattered to the hottop. The spider struck the side of a small sports car hard enough to make it rock on its springs, and then it was gone.

I got to Mrs. Reppler, who was swaying on her feet and dead pale. I put an arm around her. "Thank you, young man," she said. "I feel a bit faint."

"That's okay," I said hoarsely.

"I would have saved him if I could."

"I know that."

Ollie joined us. We ran for the market doors, the threads falling all around us. One lit on Mrs. Reppler's marketing basket and sank into the canvas side. She tussled grimly for what was hers, dragging back on the strap with both hands, but she lost it. It went bumping off into the mist, end over end.

As we reached the IN door, a smaller spider, no bigger than a cocker spaniel puppy, raced out of the fog along the side of the building. It was producing no webbing; perhaps it wasn't mature enough to do so.

As Ollie leaned one beefy shoulder against the door so Mrs. Reppler could go through, I heaved the steel bar at the thing like a javelin and impaled it. It writhed madly, legs scratching at the air, and its red eyes seemed to find mine, and mark me . . .

"David!" Ollie was still holding the door.

I ran in. He followed me.

Pallid, frightened faces stared at us. Seven of us had gone out. Three of us had come back. Ollie leaned against the heavy glass door, barrel chest heaving. He began to reload Amanda's gun. His white assistant manager's shirt was plastered to his body, and large gray sweat-stains had crept out from under his arms.

"What?" someone asked in a low, hoarse voice.

"Spiders," Mrs. Reppler answered grimly. "The dirty bastards snatched my market basket."

Then Billy hurled his way into my arms, crying. I held on to him. Tight.

X

**The Spell of Mrs. Carmody.
The Second Night
in the Market.
The Final Confrontation.**

It was my turn to sleep, and for four hours I remember nothing at all. Amanda told me I talked a lot, and screamed once or twice, but I remember no dreams. When I woke up it was afternoon. I was terribly thirsty. Some of the milk had gone over, but some of it was still okay. I drank a quart.

Amanda came over to where Billy, Mrs. Turman, and I were. The old man who had offered to make a try for the shotgun in the trunk of his car was with her—Cornell, I remembered. Ambrose Cornell.

"How are you, son?" he asked.

"All right." But I was still thirsty and my head ached. Most of all, I was scared. I slipped an arm around Billy and looked from Cornell to Amanda. "What's up?"

Amanda said, "Mr. Cornell is worried about that Mrs. Carmody. So am I."

"Billy, why don't you take a walk over here with me?" Hattie asked.

"I don't want to," Billy said.

"Go on, Big Bill," I told him, and he went—reluctantly.

"Now what about Mrs. Carmody?" I asked.

"She's stirrin' things up," Cornell said. He looked at me with an old man's grimness. "I think we got to put a stop to it. Just about any way we can."

Amanda said, "There are almost a dozen people with her now. It's like some crazy kind of a church service."

I remembered talking with a writer friend who lived in Otisfield and supported his wife and two kids by raising chickens and turning out one paperback original a year—spy stories. We had gotten talking about the bulge in popularity of books concerning themselves with the supernatural. Gault pointed out that in the forties *Weird Tales* had only been able to pay a pittance, and that in the fifties it went broke. When the machines fail, he had said (while his wife candled eggs and roosters crowed querulously outside), when the technologies fail, when the conventional religious systems fail, people have got to have something. Even a zombie lurching through the night can seem pretty cheerful compared to the existential comedy/horror of the ozone layer dissolving under the combined assault of a million fluorocarbon spray cans of deodorant.

We had been trapped here for twenty-six hours and we hadn't been able to do diddlyshit. Our one expedition outside had resulted in fifty-seven percent losses. It wasn't so surprising that Mrs. Carmody had turned into a growth stock, maybe.

"Has she really got a dozen people?" I asked.

"Well, only eight," Cornell said. "But she never shuts up! It's like those ten-hour speeches Castro used to make. It's a goddamn filibuster."

Eight people. Not that many, not even enough to fill up a jury box. But I understood the worry on their faces. It was enough to make them the single largest political force in the market, especially now that Dan and Mike were gone. The thought that the biggest single group in our closed system was listening to her rant on about the pits of hell and the seven vials being opened made me feel pretty damn claustrophobic.

"She's started talking about human sacrifice again," Amanda said. "Bud Brown came over and told her to stop talking that drivel in his store. And two of the men that are with her—one of them was that man Myron LaFleur—told him he was the one who better shut up because it was still a free country. He wouldn't shut up and there was a . . . well, a shoving match, I guess you'd say."

"Brown got a bloody nose," Cornell said. "They mean business."

I said, "Surely not to the point of actually killing someone."

Cornell said softly, "I don't know how far they'll go if that mist doesn't let up. But I don't want to find out. I intend to get out of here."

"Easier said than done." But something had begun to tick over in my mind. *Scent.* That was the key. We had been left pretty much alone in the market. The bugs might have been attracted to the light, as more ordinary bugs were. The birds had simply followed their food supply. But the bigger things had left us alone unless we unbuttoned for some reason. The slaughter in the Bridgton Pharmacy had occurred because the doors had been left chocked open—I was sure of that. The thing or things that had gotten Norton and his party had sounded as big as a house, but it or they hadn't come near the market. And that meant that maybe . . .

Suddenly I wanted to talk to Ollie Weeks. I needed to talk to him.

"I intend to get out or die trying," Cornell said. "I got no plans to spend the rest of the summer in here."

"There have been four suicides," Amanda said suddenly.

"What?" The first thing to cross my mind, in a semiguilty flash, was that the bodies of the soldiers had been discovered.

"Pills," Cornell said shortly. "Me and two or three other guys carried the bodies out back."

I had to stifle a shrill laugh. We had a regular morgue going back there.

"It's thinning out," Cornell said. "I want to get gone."

"You won't make it to your car. Believe me."

"Not even to that first rank? That's closer than the drugstore."

I didn't answer him. Not then.

About an hour later I found Ollie holding up the beer cooler and drinking a Busch. His face was impassive but he also seemed to be watching Mrs. Carmody. She was tireless, apparently. And she was indeed discussing human sacrifice again, only now no one was telling her to shut up. Some of the people who had told her to shut up yesterday were either with her today or at least willing to listen—and the others were outnumbered.

"She could have them talked around to it by tomorrow morning," Ollie remarked. "Maybe not . . . but if she did, who do you think she'd single out for the honor?"

Bud Brown had crossed her. So had Amanda. There was the man who had struck her. And then, of course, there was me.

"Ollie," I said, "I think maybe half a dozen of us could get out of here. I don't know how far we'd get, but I think we could at least get out."

"How?"

I laid it out for him. It was simple enough. If we dashed across to my Scout and piled in, they would get no human scent. At least not with the windows rolled up.

"But suppose they're attracted to some other scent?" Ollie asked. "Exhaust, for instance?"

"Then we'd be cooked," I agreed.

"Motion," he said. "The motion of a car through fog might also draw them, David."

"I don't think so. Not without the scent of prey. I really believe that's the key to getting away."

"But you don't know."

"No, not for sure."

"Where would you want to go?"

"First? Home. To get my wife."

"David—"

"All right. To check. To be *sure.*"

"The things out there could be everyplace, David. They could get you the minute you stepped out of your Scout into your dooryard."

"If that happened, the Scout would be yours. All I'd ask would be that you take care of Billy as well as you could for as long as you could."

Ollie finished his Busch and dropped the can back into the cooler, where it clattered among the empties. The butt of the gun Amanda's husband had given her protruded from his pocket.

"South?" he asked, meeting my eyes.

"Yeah, I would," I said. "Go south and try to get out of the mist. Try like hell."

"How much gas you got?"

"Almost full."

"Have you thought that it might be impossible to get out?"

I had. Suppose what they had been fooling with at the Arrowhead Project had pulled this entire region into another dimension as easily as you or I would turn a sock inside out? "It had crossed my mind," I said, "but the alternative seems to be waiting around to see who Mrs. Carmody taps for the place of honor."

"Were you thinking about today?"

"No, it's afternoon already and those things get active at night. I was thinking about tomorrow, very early."

"Who would you want to take?"

"Me and you and Billy. Hattie Turman. Amanda Dumfries. That old guy Cornell and Mrs. Reppler. Maybe Bud Brown, too. That's eight, but Billy can sit on someone's lap and we can all squash together."

He thought it over. "All right," he said finally. "We'll try. Have you mentioned this to anyone else?"

"No, not yet."

"My advice would be not to, not until about four tomorrow morning. I'll put a couple of bags of groceries under the checkout nearest the door. If we're lucky we can squeak out before anyone knows what's happening." His eyes drifted to Mrs. Carmody again. "If she knew, she might try to stop us."

"You think so?"

Ollie got another beer. "I think so," he said.

That afternoon—yesterday afternoon—passed in a kind of slow motion. Darkness crept in, turning the fog to that dull chrome color again. What world was left outside slowly dissolved to black by eight-thirty.

The pink bugs returned, then the bird-things, swooping into the windows and scooping them up. Something roared occasionally from the dark, and once, shortly before midnight, there was a long, drawn-out *Aaaaa-rooooooo!* that caused people to turn toward the blackness with frightened, searching faces. It was the sort of sound you'd imagine a bull alligator might make in a swamp.

It went pretty much as Miller had predicted. By the small hours, Mrs. Carmody had gained another half a dozen souls. Mr. McVey the butcher was among them, standing with his arms folded, watching her.

She was totally wound up. She seemed to need no sleep. Her sermon, a steady stream of horrors out of Doré, Bosch, and Jonathan Edwards, went on and on, building toward some climax. Her group began to murmur with her, to rock back and forth unconsciously, like true believers at a tent revival. Their eyes were shiny and blank. They were under her spell.

Around 3:00 A.M. (the sermon went on relentlessly, and the people who were not interested had retreated to the back to try to get some sleep), I saw Ollie put a bag of groceries on a shelf under the checkout nearest the OUT door. Half an hour later he put another bag beside it. No one appeared to notice him but me. Billy, Amanda, and Mrs. Turman slept together by the denuded cold-cuts section. I joined them and fell into an uneasy doze.

At four-fifteen by my wristwatch, Ollie shook me awake. Cornell was with him, his eyes gleaming brightly from behind his spectacles.

"It's time, David," Ollie said.

A nervous cramp hit my belly and then passed. I shook Amanda awake. The question of what might happen with both Amanda and Stephanie in the car together passed into my mind, and then passed right out again. Today it would be best to take things just as they came.

Those remarkable green eyes opened and looked into mine. "David?"

"We're going to take a stab at getting out of here. Do you want to come?"

"What are you talking about?"

I started to explain, then woke up Mrs. Turman so I would only have to go through it the once.

"Your theory about scent," Amanda said. "It's really only an educated guess at this point, isn't it?"

"Yes."

"It doesn't matter to me," Hattie said. Her face was white and in spite of the sleep she'd gotten there were large discolored patches under her eyes. "I would do anything—take any chances—just to see the sun again."

Just to see the sun again. A little shiver coursed through me. She had put her finger on a spot that was very close to the center of my own fears, on the sense of almost foregone doom that had gripped me since I had seen Norm dragged out through the loading door. You could only see the sun through the mist as a little silver coin. It was like being on Venus.

It wasn't so much the monstrous creatures that lurked in the mist; my shot with the pinchbar had shown me they were no Lovecraftian horrors with immortal life but only organic creatures with their own vulnerabilities. It was the mist itself that sapped the strength and robbed the will. *Just to see the sun again.* She was right. That alone would be worth going through a lot of hell.

I smiled at Hattie and she smiled tentatively back.

"Yes," Amanda said. "Me too."

I began to shake Billy awake as gently as I could.

"I'm with you," Mrs. Reppler said briefly.

We were all together by the meat counter, all but Bud Brown. He had thanked us for the invitation and then declined it. He would not leave his place in the market, he said, but added in a remarkably gentle tone of voice that he didn't blame Ollie for doing so.

An unpleasant, sweetish aroma was beginning to drift up from the white enamel case now, a smell that reminded me of the time our freezer went on the fritz while we were spending a week on the Cape. Perhaps, I thought, it was the smell of spoiling meat that had driven Mr. McVey over to Mrs. Carmody's team.

"—*expiation! It's expiation we want to think about now! We have been scourged with whips and scorpions! We have been punished for delving into secrets forbidden by God of old! We have seen the lips of the earth open! We have seen the obscenities of nightmare! The rock will not hide them, the dead tree gives no shelter! And how will it end? What will stop it?"*

"*Expiation!*" shouted good old Myron LaFleur.

"Expiation . . . expiation . . ." They whispered it uncertainly.

"Let me hear you say it like you mean it!" Mrs. Carmody shouted. The veins stood out on her neck in bulging cords. Her voice was cracking and hoarse now, but still full of power. And it occurred to me that it was the mist that had given her that power—the power to cloud men's minds, to make a particularly apt pun—just as it had taken away the sun's power from the rest of us. Before, she had been nothing but a mildly eccentric old woman with an antiques store in a town that was lousy with antiques stores. Nothing but an old woman with a few stuffed animals in the back room and a reputation for

(that witch . . . that cunt)

folk medicine. It was said she could find water with an applewood stick, that she could charm warts, and sell you a cream that would fade freckles to shadows of their former selves. I had even heard—was it from old Bill Giosti?—that Mrs. Carmody could be seen (in total confidence) about your love life; that if you were having the bedroom miseries, she could give you a drink that would put the ram back in your rod.

"EXPIATION!" they all cried together.

"Expiation, that's right!" she shouted deliriously. *"It's expiation gonna clear away this fog! Expiation gonna clear off these monsters and abominations! Expiation gonna drop the scales of mist from our eyes and let us see!"* Her voice dropped a notch. *"And what does the*

Bible say expiation is? What is the only cleanser for sin in the Eye and Mind of God?"

"Blood."

This time the chill shuddered up through my entire body, cresting at the nape of my neck and making the hairs there stiffen. Mr. McVey had spoken that word, Mr. McVey the butcher who had been cutting meat in Bridgton ever since I was a kid holding my father's talented hand. Mr. McVey taking orders and cutting meat in his stained whites. Mr. McVey, whose acquaintanceship with the knife was long—yes, and with the saw and cleaver as well. Mr. McVey who would understand better than anyone else that the cleanser of the soul flows from the wounds of the body.

"Blood . . ." they whispered.

"Daddy, I'm scared," Billy said. He was clutching my hand tightly, his small face strained and pale.

"Ollie," I said, "why don't we get out of this loony bin?"

"Right on," he said. "Let's go."

We started down the second aisle in a loose group—Ollie, Amanda, Cornell, Mrs. Turman, Mrs. Reppler, Billy, and I. It was a quarter to five in the morning and the mist was beginning to lighten again.

"You and Cornell take the grocery bags," Ollie said to me.

"Okay."

"I'll go first. Your Scout is a four-door, is it?"

"Yeah. It is."

"Okay, I'll open the driver's door and the back

door on the same side. Mrs. Dumfries, can you carry Billy?"

She picked him up in her arms.

"Am I too heavy?" Billy asked.

"No, hon."

"Good."

"You and Billy get in front," Ollie went on. "Shove way over. Mrs. Turman in front, in the middle. David, you behind the wheel. The rest of us will—"

"Where did you think you were going?"

It was Mrs. Carmody.

She stood at the head of the checkout line where Ollie had hidden the bags of groceries. Her pantsuit was a yellow scream in the gloom. Her hair frizzed out wildly in all directions, reminding me momentarily of Elsa Lanchester in *The Bride of Frankenstein*. Her eyes blazed. Ten or fifteen people stood behind her, blocking the IN and OUT doors. They had the look of people who had been in car accidents, or who had seen a UFO land, or who had seen a tree pull its roots up and walk.

Billy cringed against Amanda and buried his face against her neck.

"Going out now, Mrs. Carmody," Ollie said. His voice was curiously gentle. "Stand away, please."

"You can't go out. That way is death. Don't you know that by now?"

"No one has interfered with you," I said. "All we want is the same privilege."

She bent and found the bags of groceries unerringly. She must have known what we were planning all along. She pulled them out from the shelf where Ollie had placed them. One ripped open, spilling cans across the floor. She threw the other and it smashed open with the sound of breaking glass. Soda ran fizzing every which way and sprayed off the chrome facing of the next checkout lane.

"These are the sort of people who brought it on!" she shouted. "People who will not bend to the will of the Almighty! Sinners in pride, haughty they are, and stiff-necked! It is from their number that the sacrifice must come! *From their number the blood of expiation!*"

A rising rumble of agreement spurred her on. She was in a frenzy now. Spittle flew from her lips as she screamed at the people crowding up behind her: *"It's the boy we want! Grab him! Take him! It's the boy we want!"*

They surged forward, Myron LaFleur in the lead, his eyes blankly joyous. Mr. McVey was directly behind him, his face blank and stolid.

Amanda faltered backward, holding Billy more tightly. His arms were wrapped around her neck. She looked at me, terrified. "David, what do I—"

"Get them both!" Mrs. Carmody screamed. *"Get his whore, too!"*

She was an apocalypse of yellow and dark joy. Her purse was still over her arm. She began to jump up and down. *"Get the boy, get the whore, get them both, get them all, get—"*

A single sharp report rang out.

Everything froze, as if we were a classroom full of

unruly children and the teacher had just stepped back in and shut the door sharply. Myron LaFleur and Mr. McVey stopped where they were, about ten paces away. Myron looked back uncertainly at the butcher. He didn't look back or even seem to realize that LaFleur was there. Mr. McVey had a look I had seen on too many other faces in the last two days. He had gone over. His mind had snapped.

Myron backed up, staring at Ollie Weeks with widening, fearful eyes. His backing-up became a run. He turned the corner of the aisle, skidded on a can, fell down, scrambled up again, and was gone.

Ollie stood in the classic target shooter's position, Amanda's gun clasped in both hands. Mrs. Carmody still stood at the head of the checkout lane. Both of her liver-spotted hands were clasped over her stomach. Blood poured out between her fingers and splashed her yellow slacks.

Her mouth opened and closed. Once. Twice. She was trying to talk. At last she made it.

"You will all die out there," she said, and then she pitched slowly forward. Her purse slithered off her arm, struck the floor, and spilled its contents. A paper-wrapped tube rolled across the distance between us and struck one of my shoes. Without thinking, I bent over and picked it up. It was a half-used package of Rolaids. I threw it down again. I didn't want to touch anything that belonged to her.

The "congregation" was backing away, spreading out, their focus broken. None of them took their eyes from the fallen figure and the dark blood spreading out from beneath her body. "You murdered her!" someone cried out in fear and anger. But no one pointed out that she had been planning something similar for my son.

Ollie was still frozen in his shooter's position, but now his mouth was trembling. I touched him gently. "Ollie, let's go. And thank you."

"I killed her," he said hoarsely. "Damn if I didn't kill her."

"Yes," I said. "That's why I thanked you. Now let's go."

We began to move again.

With no grocery bags to carry—thanks to Mrs. Carmody—I was able to take Billy. We paused for a moment at the door, and Ollie said in a low, strained voice, "I wouldn't have shot her, David. Not if there had been any other way."

"Yeah."

"You believe it?"

"Yeah, I do."

"Then let's go."

We went out.

XI

The End.

Ollie moved fast, the pistol in his right hand. Before Billy and I were more than out the door he was at my Scout, an insubstantial Ollie, like a ghost in a television movie. He opened the driver's door. Then the back door. Then something came out of the mist and cut him nearly in half.

I never got a good look at it, and for that I think I'm grateful. It appeared to be red, the angry color of a cooked lobster. It had claws. It was making a low grunting sound, not much different from the sound we had heard after Norton and his little band of Flat-Earthers went out.

Ollie got off one shot, and then the thing's claws scissored forward and Ollie's body seemed to un-hinge in a terrible glut of blood. Amanda's gun fell out of his hand, struck the pavement, and dis-charged. I caught a nightmare glimpse of huge black lusterless eyes, the size of giant handfuls of sea grapes, and then the thing lurched back into the mist with what remained of Ollie Weeks in its grip. A long, multisegmented scorpion's body dragged harshly on the paving.

There was an instant of choices. Maybe there always is, no matter how short. Half of me wanted to run back into the market with Billy hugged to my chest. The other half was racing for the Scout, throwing Billy inside, lunging after him. Then Amanda screamed. It was a high, rising sound that seemed to spiral up and up until it was nearly ultrasonic. Billy cringed against me, digging his face against my chest.

One of the spiders had Hattie Turman. It was big. It had knocked her down. Her dress had pulled up over her scrawny knees as it crouched over her, its bristly, spiny legs caressing her shoulders. It began to spin its web.

Mrs. Carmody was right, I thought. *We're going to die out here, we are really going to die out here.*

"Amanda!" I yelled.

No response. She was totally gone. The spider straddled what remained of Billy's babysitter, who had enjoyed jigsaw puzzles and those damned Double-Crostics that no normal person can do without going nuts. Its threads crisscrossed her body, the white strands already turning red as the acid coating sank into her.

Cornell was backing slowly toward the market, his eyes as big as dinner plates behind his specs. Abruptly he turned and ran. He clawed the IN door open and ran inside.

The split in my mind closed as Mrs. Reppler stepped briskly forward and slapped Amanda, first forehand, then backhand. Amanda stopped screaming. I went to her, spun her around to face the Scout, and screamed "GO!" into her face.

She went. Mrs. Reppler brushed past me. She pushed Amanda into the Scout's backseat, got in after her, and slammed the door shut.

I yanked Billy loose and threw him in. As I climbed in myself, one of those spider threads drifted down and lit on my ankle. It burned the way a fishing line pulled rapidly through your closed fist will burn. And it was strong. I gave my foot a hard yank and it broke. I slipped in behind the wheel.

"Shut it, oh shut the door, dear God!" Amanda screamed.

I shut the door. A bare instant later, one of the spiders thumped softly against it. I was only inches from its red, viciously stupid eyes. Its legs, each as thick as my wrist, slipped back and forth across the square bonnet. Amanda screamed ceaselessly, like a firebell.

"Woman, shut your head," Mrs. Reppler told her.

The spider gave up. It could not smell us, ergo we were no longer there. It strutted back into the mist on its unsettling number of legs, became a phantasm, and then was gone.

I looked out the window to make sure it was gone and then opened the door.

"What are you doing?" Amanda screamed, but I knew what I was doing. I like to think Ollie would

have done exactly the same thing. I half-stepped, half-leaned out, and got the gun. Something came rapidly toward me, but I never saw it. I pulled back in and slammed the door shut.

Amanda began to sob. Mrs. Reppler put an arm around her and comforted her briskly.

Billy said, "Are we going home, Daddy?"

"Big Bill, we're gonna try."

"Okay," he said quietly.

I checked the gun and then put it into the glove compartment. Ollie had reloaded it after the expedition to the drugstore. The rest of the shells had disappeared with him, but that was all right. He had fired at Mrs. Carmody, he had fired once at the clawed thing, and the gun had discharged once when it hit the ground. There were four of us in the Scout, but if push came right down to shove, I'd find some other way out for myself.

I had a terrible moment when I couldn't find my key ring. I checked all my pockets, came up empty, and then checked them all again, forcing myself to go slowly and calmly. They were in my jeans pocket; they had gotten down under the coins, as keys sometimes will. The Scout started easily. At the confident roar of the engine, Amanda burst into fresh tears.

I sat there, letting it idle, waiting to see what was going to be drawn by the sound of the engine or the smell of the exhaust. Five minutes, the longest five of my life, drifted by. Nothing happened.

"Are we going to sit here or are we going to go?" Mrs. Reppler asked at last.

"Go," I said. I backed out of the slot and put on the low beams.

Some urge—probably a base one—made me cruise past the Federal market as close as I could get. The Scout's right bumper bunted the trash barrel to one side. It was impossible to see in except through the loopholes—all those fertilizer and lawn-food bags made the place look as if it were in the throes of some mad garden sale—but at each loophole there were two or three pale faces, staring out at us.

Then I swung to the left, and the mist closed impenetrably behind us. And what has become of those people I do not know.

I drove back down Kansas Road at five miles an hour, feeling my way. Even with the Scout's headlights and running lights on, it was impossible to see more than seven or ten feet ahead.

The earth had been through some terrible contortion; Miller had been right about that. In places the road was merely cracked, but in others the ground itself seemed to have caved in, tilting up great slabs of paving. I was able to get over with the help of the four-wheel drive. Thank God for that. But I was terribly afraid that we would soon come to an obstacle that even the four-wheel drive couldn't get us over.

It took me forty minutes to make a drive that usually only took seven or eight. At last the sign that marked our private road loomed out of the mist.

Billy, roused at a quarter of five, had fallen solidly asleep inside this car that he knew so well it must have seemed like home to him.

Amanda looked at the road nervously. "Are you really going down there?"

"I'm going to try," I said.

But it was impossible. The storm that had whipped through had loosened a lot of trees, and that weird, twisting drop had finished the job of tumbling them. I was able to crunch over the first two; they were fairly small. Then I came to a hoary old pine lying across the road like an outlaw's barricade. It was still almost a quarter of a mile to the house. Billy slept on beside me, and I put the Scout in Park, put my hands over my eyes, and tried to think what to do next.

Now, as I sit in the Howard Johnson's near Exit 3 of the Maine Turnpike, writing all of this down on HoJo stationery, I suspect that Mrs. Reppler, that tough and capable old broad, could have laid out the essential futility of the situation in a few quick strokes. But she had the kindness to let me think it through for myself.

I couldn't get out. I couldn't leave them. I couldn't even kid myself that all the horror-movie monsters were back at the Federal; when I cracked the window I could hear them in the woods, crashing and blundering around on the steep fall of land they call the Ledges around these parts. The moisture drip-drip-dripped from the overhanging leaves. Overhead the mist darkened momentarily as some nightmarish and half-seen living kite overflew us.

I tried to tell myself—then and now—that if she was very quick, if she buttoned up the house with herself inside, that she had enough food for ten days to two weeks. It only works a little bit. What keeps getting in the way is my last memory of her, wearing her floppy sunhat and gardening gloves, on her way to our little vegetable patch with the mist rolling inexorably across the lake behind her.

It is Billy I have to think about now. Billy, I tell myself. Big Bill, Big Bill . . . I should write it maybe a hundred times on this sheet of paper, like a child condemned to write *I will not throw spitballs in school* as the sunny three-o'clock stillness spills through the windows and the teacher corrects homework papers at her desk and the only sound is her pen, while somewhere, far away, kids pick up teams for scratch baseball.

Anyway, at last I did the only thing I could do. I reversed the Scout carefully back to Kansas Road. Then I cried.

Amanda touched my shoulder timidly. "David, I'm so sorry," she said.

"Yeah," I said, trying to stop the tears and not having much luck. "Yeah, so am I."

I drove to Route 302 and turned left, toward Portland. This road was also cracked and blasted in places, but was, on the whole, more passable than Kansas Road had been. I was worried about the bridges. The face of Maine is cut with running water, and there are bridges everywhere, big and small. But the Naples Causeway was intact, and from there it was plain—if slow—sailing all the way to Portland.

The mist held thick. Once I had to stop, thinking that trees were lying across the road. Then the trees began to move and undulate and I understood they were more tentacles. I stopped, and after a while they drew back. Once a great green thing with an iridescent green body and long transparent wings landed on the hood. It looked like a grossly misshapen dragonfly. It hovered there for a moment, then took wing again and was gone.

Billy woke up about two hours after we had left Kansas Road behind and asked if we had gotten Mommy yet. I told him I hadn't been able to get down our road because of fallen trees.

"Is she all right, Dad?"

"Billy, I don't know. But we'll come back and see."

He didn't cry. He dozed off again instead. I would have rather had his tears. He was sleeping too damn much and I didn't like it.

I began to get a tension headache. It was driving through the fog at a steady five or ten miles an hour that did it, the tension of knowing that anything might come out of it, anything at all—a washout, a landspill, or Ghidra the Three-headed Monster. I think I prayed. I prayed to God that Stephanie was alive and that He wouldn't take my adultery out on her. I prayed to God to let me get Billy to safety because he had been through so much.

Most people had pulled to the side of the road when the mist came, and by noon we were in North Windham. I tried the River Road, but about four miles down, a bridge spanning a small and noisy stream had fallen into the water. I had to reverse for nearly a mile before I found a spot wide enough to turn around. We went to Portland by Route 302 after all.

When we got there, I drove the cutoff to the turnpike. The neat line of tollbooths guarding the access had been turned into vacant-eyed skeletons of smashed Pola-Glas. All of them were empty. In the sliding glass doorway of one was a torn jacket with Maine Turnpike Authority patches on the sleeves. It was drenched with tacky, drying blood. We had not seen a single living person since leaving the Federal.

Mrs. Reppler said, "David, try your radio."

I slapped my forehead in frustration and anger at myself, wondering how I could have been stupid enough to forget the Scout's AM/FM for so long.

"Don't do that," Mrs. Reppler said curtly. "You can't think of everything. If you try, you will go mad and be of no use at all."

I got nothing but a shriek of static all the way across the AM band, and the FM yielded nothing but a smooth and ominous silence.

"Does that mean everything's off the air?" Amanda asked. I knew what she was thinking, maybe. We were far enough south now so that we should have been picking up a selection of strong Boston stations—WRKO, WBZ, WMEX. But if Boston had gone—

"It doesn't mean anything for sure," I said. "That static on the AM band is pure interference. The mist is having a damping effect on radio signals, too."

"Are you sure that's all it is?"

"Yes," I said, not sure at all.

We went south. The mileposts rolled past, counting down from about forty. When we reached Mile 1, we would be at the New Hampshire border. Going on the turnpike was slower; a lot of the drivers hadn't wanted to give up, and there had been rear-end collisions in several places. Several times I had to use the median strip.

At about twenty past one—I was beginning to feel hungry—Billy clutched my arm. "Daddy, what's that? *What's that!*"

A shadow loomed out of the mist, staining it dark. It was as tall as a cliff and coming right at us. I jammed on the brakes. Amanda, who had been cat-napping, was thrown forward.

Something came; again, that is all I can say for sure. It may have been the fact that the mist only allowed us to glimpse things briefly, but I think it just as likely that there are certain things that your brain simply disallows. There are things of such darkness and horror—just, I suppose, as there are things of such great beauty—that they will not fit through the puny human doors of perception.

It was six-legged, I know that; its skin was slaty gray that mottled to dark brown in places. Those brown patches reminded me absurdly of the liver spots on Mrs. Carmody's hands. Its skin was deeply wrinkled and grooved, and clinging to it were scores, hundreds, of those pinkish "bugs" with the stalk-eyes. I don't know how big it actually was, but it passed directly over us. One of its gray, wrinkled legs smashed down right beside my window, and Mrs. Reppler said later she could not see the under-side of its body, although she craned her neck up to look. She saw only two Cyclopean legs going up and up into the mist like living towers until they were lost to sight.

For the moment it was over the Scout I had an impression of something so big that it might have made a blue whale look the size of a trout—in other words, something so big that it defied the imagina-tion. Then it was gone, sending a seismological series of thuds back. It left tracks in the cement of the Inter-state, tracks so deep I could not see the bottoms. Each single track was nearly big enough to drop the Scout into.

For a moment no one spoke. There was no sound but our breathing and the diminishing thud of that great Thing's passage.

Then Billy said, "Was it a dinosaur, Dad? Like the bird that got into the market?"

"I don't think so. I don't think there was ever an animal that big, Billy. At least not on earth."

I thought of the Arrowhead Project and wondered again what crazy damned thing they could have been doing up there.

"Can we go on?" Amanda asked timidly. "It might come back."

Yes, and there might be more up ahead. But there was no point in saying so. We had to go somewhere. I drove on, weaving in and out between those terrible tracks until they veered off the road.

That is what happened. Or nearly all—there is one final thing I'll get to in a moment. But you mustn't expect some neat conclusion. There is no *And they escaped from the mist into the good sunshine of a new day;* or *When we awoke the National Guard had finally arrived;* or even that great old standby: *It was all a dream.*

It is, I suppose, what my father always frowningly called "an Alfred Hitchcock ending," by which he meant a conclusion in ambiguity that allowed the reader or viewer to make up his own mind about how things ended. My father had nothing but contempt for such stories, saying they were "cheap shots."

We got to this Howard Johnson's near Exit 3 as dusk began to close in, making driving a suicidal risk. Before that, we took a chance on the bridge that spans the Saco River. It looked badly twisted out of shape, but in the mist it was impossible to tell if it was whole or not. That particular game we won.

But there's tomorrow to think of, isn't there?

As I write this, it is a quarter to one in the morning, July the twenty-third. The storm that seemed to signal the beginning of it all was only four days ago. Billy is sleeping in the lobby on a mattress that I dragged out for him. Amanda and Mrs. Reppler are close by. I am writing by the light of a big Delco flashlight, and outside the pink bugs are ticking and thumping off the glass. Every now and then there is a louder thud as one of the birds takes one off.

The Scout has enough gas to take us maybe another ninety miles. The alternative is to try to gas up here; there is an Exxon out on the service island, and although the power is off, I believe I could siphon some up from the tank. But—

But it means being outside.

If we can get gas—here or further along—we'll keep going. I have a destination in mind now, you see. It's that last thing I wanted to tell you about.

I couldn't be sure. That is the thing, the damned thing. It might have been my imagination, nothing but wish fulfillment. And even if not, it is such a long chance. How many miles? How many bridges? How many things that would love to tear up my son and eat him even as he screamed in terror and agony?

The chances are so good that it was nothing but a daydream that I haven't told the others . . . at least, not yet.

In the manager's apartment I found a large battery-operated multiband radio. From the back of it, a flat antenna wire led out through the window. I turned it on, switched over to BAT., fiddled with the tuning dial, with the SQUELCH knob, and still got nothing but static or dead silence.

And then, at the far end of the AM band, just as I was reaching for the knob to turn it off, I thought I heard, or dreamed I heard, one single word.

There was no more. I listened for an hour, but there was no more. If there was that one word, it came through some minute shift in the damping mist, an infinitesimal break that immediately closed again.

One word.

I've got to get some sleep . . . if I can sleep and not be haunted until daybreak by the faces of Ollie Weeks and Mrs. Carmody and Norm the bag-boy . . . and by Steff's face, half-shadowed by the wide brim of her sunhat.

There is a restaurant here, a typical HoJo restaurant with a dining room and a long, horseshoe-shaped lunch counter. I am going to leave these pages on the counter and perhaps someday someone will find them and read them.

One word.

If I only really heard it. If only.

I'm going to bed now. But first I'm going to kiss my son and whisper two words in his ear. Against the dreams that may come, you know.

Two words that sound a bit alike.

One of them is Hartford.

The other is hope.

Stephen King

SKELETON CREW

TWENTY-TWO STORIES FROM THE
#1 BESTSELLING AUTHOR

In this brilliant collection of stories,
Stephen King takes readers down
paths that only he could imagine....

A supermarket becomes the place
where humanity takes its last stand
against unholy destruction...
a trip to the attic turns into a
journey to hell...a woman driver
finds a scary shortcut to paradise...
an idyllic lake harbors a bottomless
evil...and a desert island is the scene
of the most terrifying struggle for
survival ever waged.

The Epic World of Stephen King

THE DARK TOWER Series
begins with...

THE GUNSLINGER *The Dark Tower I*
"The man in black fled across the desert, and the gunslinger followed." So begins the saga of Roland, the Last Gunslinger, and the epic journey that will take him to the end of this world—and others.

THE DRAWING OF THE THREE
The Dark Tower II
After his confrontation with the man in black at the end of *The Gunslinger*, Roland awakes to find three doors on the beach of Mid-World's Western Sea—each leading to New York City but at three different moments in time. Through these doors, Roland must "draw" three figures crucial to his quest for the Dark Tower.

THE WASTE LANDS *The Dark Tower III*
Roland, the Last Gunslinger, moves ever closer to the Dark Tower of his dreams and nightmares—as he crosses a land of damnation in a macabre world that is a twisted mirror image of our own.

WIZARD AND GLASS *The Dark Tower IV*
Roland tells his fellow adventurers a tale of spellbinding magic, long-ago love and supreme menace. With his story told, their journey to the tower takes them to the realm of the Crimson King, and in the chambers of the villain, Flagg.

BEYOND THE DARK TOWER
WHERE THE
SHADOWS CRAWL...

Stephen King's
Masterworks Live On

THE STAND
The evil started in a laboratory and took over America. Those who died quickly were the lucky ones. Something terrifying was waiting to claim the few scattered survivors—and a final battle between good and evil is all that separates him from reaching for their very souls...

THE EYES OF THE DRAGON
The ultimate in dark enchantment. In the kingdom of Delain, wickedness drips from the palace walls as the heir to the throne must do battle with the evil wizard Flagg, and his pawn, the younger Prince Thomas. A classic fairy tale twisted into a masterpiece of fiction.

INSOMNIA
Ralph Roberts lies silently, eyes shut, waiting for the inevitable—but insomnia has robbed him of his sleep. Now Ralph's eyes are wide open—cursed by the vision of horrible things befalling the people of Derry, all under the watchful gaze of the Crimson King. Ralph can see the truth, and it just might kill him.